His voice was as soft as a caress. . . .

As he spoke he twisted a strand of hair around his fingers, sending more shivers up her back. He kissed the base of her neck and it took away her breath. He kissed her shoulder and then ran a finger down the center of her back, something she could not possibly ignore.

She didn't want him to touch her, Lisbeth told herself. She didn't want him to make her feel this way. And so she would tell him. But when she spoke, her voice did not sound very much like itself.

"Stop!" was scarcely a whisper.

"Do you really want me to do so?" he asked.

Thomas leaned over her so that she could not evade his gaze. He was smiling but his eyes were serious, demanding honesty. And it was honesty that Lisbeth found she could not deny him.

"I don't know what I wish," she confessed. "When you touch me like this my senses are all disarrayed. I like it, and yet I cannot help but feel it keeps us from talking about the things that matter."

"This," he said, kissing her, "is what matters. And this," he added, touching the creamy skin of her throat at the neckline of her night shift.

Suddenly Lisbeth found she no longer wished to argue. . . .

The
Soldier's Bride

April Kihlstrom

A SIGNET BOOK

SIGNET
Published by New American Library, a division of
Penguin Putnam Inc., 375 Hudson Street,
New York, New York 10014, U.S.A.
Penguin Books Ltd, 80 Strand,
London WC2R 0RL, England
Penguin Books Australia Ltd, Ringwood,
Victoria, Australia
Penguin Books Canada Ltd, 10 Alcorn Avenue,
Toronto, Ontario, Canada M4V 3B2
Penguin Books (N.Z.) Ltd, 182-190 Wairau Road,
Auckland 10, New Zealand

Penguin Books Ltd, Registered Offices:
Harmondsworth, Middlesex, England

First published by Signet, an imprint of New American Library,
a division of Penguin Putnam Inc.

First Printing, February 2002
10 9 8 7 6 5 4 3 2 1

In memory of Ellen Hammer. She taught me
to follow my hopes and dreams.
I will miss her.

Chapter 1

Lisbeth Barlow stared out the window of her sister's London town house at the summer rain. Her mood was as unsettled as the weather. Soon she and Aunt Margaret would have to go back to Henley Hall and her emotions were as wild as the storm.

It was one thing to live at Henley Hall when her sisters were with her. It was another thing entirely when Lisbeth would be there by herself, for Aunt Margaret had already said that she wanted to return to her cottage in the woods.

Not only wouldn't Lisbeth have the people she loved most in the world with her, but she wouldn't even have the children her aunt and sister had rescued to keep her company, for they were gone as well. Lisbeth would truly be alone.

Aunt Margaret came to stand beside her. "You don't wish to leave London, do you?" she asked her niece.

Lisbeth hesitated. "I suppose we must. We cannot stay here forever, trespassing on Alex and Sir Robert's kindness. Tessa not only published her book, but she is married, and the Season is over, so there is no reason for either of us to stay here any longer, is there?"

If she heard a note of hope, almost a plea in Lisbeth's voice, Miss Winsham did not say so. In any event, what could she have replied? She was impatient to return home to her cottage. There, she could go back to doing what she loved best—healing those who were hurt or ill and rescuing children. Here in London her attempts to do so had ended in disaster. No, even though she understood Lisbeth's sentiments, Miss Winsham could not agree to stay here much longer.

But just as Aunt Margaret opened her mouth to say so, she felt something grow warm under the hand she had placed on the table by the window. She lifted her hand and started in surprise at the sight of a locket there. A grim smile tugged at the corners of her mouth. If the past were anything to go by, this would alter everything.

So instead of speaking about going back to Henley Hall, Miss Winsham handed the locket over to her niece. "Here," she said. "This is yours now. It was your mother's, then mine. As you know, Alexandra and Theresa have each had their turn with it, and now it is yours. It has been handed down, mother to daughter and sister to sister, in our family for as long as anyone can remember."

Lisbeth hesitated. She took the locket and turned it over to read the inscription aloud—just as her sisters had done before her. "Wish Always With Love."

Oh, yes, she had heard the stories from both Alex and Tessa. Now she looked at her aunt and said, "So I am supposed to see the face of my future husband here?"

"Don't ask me!" Aunt Margaret snapped in return. "Your sisters said they did, but all I can say for certain is that the thing is cunningly made and who knows what it means if you think you see a face?" She paused and her voice softened. "No one knows where the locket came from or how it works its magic. I cannot tell you whether or not it shows the face of one's true love. I never met the man whose face *I* saw."

"But that is the legend?"

"Yes, that is the legend," Miss Winsham reluctantly agreed.

Lisbeth hesitated again, but she opened the locket. And she did see a face. At least she thought she did. She even thought she knew who it was. Lord Thomas Kepley looked just like this. He had the same boyish face and golden hair and a mischievous glint in his blue eyes.

But it was nonsense, all nonsense! Lisbeth told herself as she snapped shut the locket. It must be her imagination! Though mind you, if there were a man she would ever agree to marry, it would be someone like Kepley. He was kind and gentle, despite being a soldier. And he talked with her. He confided in her and listened to what she told him. He didn't simply flirt and offer her Spanish coin like most of the men Lisbeth had met here in London.

But Kepley didn't want to marry. He was as confirmed a bachelor as she was a spinster. He had done his best to appear so wild that no mother would want him for her daughter. But of course it didn't really work that way. Not when so many young ladies thought him so dashing.

His father, the Marquess of Aylsham, had retaliated by purchasing him colors. The only reason Kepley was home at the moment was that he had sustained an injury in the Peninsula and he was back in England to recover. But he was up and about now and would soon be going to rejoin Wellington's army.

And so, face or no face in the locket, it was pointless to even consider that he might wish to marry *her*. Particularly when Lisbeth didn't wish to get married, either. Surely, she told herself, it was simply wishful thinking to believe it was his face she had seen in the locket.

"Unsuitable, is he?" Miss Winsham asked with a knowing expression upon her face.

Lisbeth started. She ought to have known that Aunt Margaret would guess far too much! There were some who even said she was a witch.

"Very unsuitable," Lisbeth agreed, though she knew there were many who would disagree, who would consider Kepley very eligible indeed.

Miss Winsham nodded brusquely. "So was the fellow your mother saw. Pity she married your father instead.

But then, Papa wouldn't listen when she tried to tell him who she loved. Nor would my father have listened to any nonsense about a locket. Of course, in my opinion, my sister would have been better off never to have married at all!"

Lisbeth took a deep breath to agree, but before she could do so Stamford's majordomo announced that a visitor had come to call.

"Lord Thomas Kepley."

Miss Winsham nudged Lisbeth, who stood there gaping. The younger woman hastily fastened the locket around her neck as she turned to greet their caller. She didn't get the chance, for her aunt spoke first.

"What the devil are you doing here?" Miss Winsham demanded bluntly as Kepley stepped into the room. "It ain't the proper hour for morning calls."

The young man flushed but fixed his gaze firmly on Lisbeth's face. "I beg pardon, but the urgency of my situation must override such considerations."

"Oh, it must, must it?"

Kepley ignored the older woman. To Lisbeth he said, "I came to ask, Miss Barlow, if you would do me the honor to become my wife."

Now it was Aunt Margaret's turn to gape. As for Lisbeth, she could do no more than drop down into the nearest chair and stare up at him, blinking.

Kepley flushed again, but it was clear he was determined to be heard. "I am being sent to rejoin Wellington's staff. I leave the day after tomorrow. In my pocket, I have a special license that would allow us to be married at once."

He paused, looked away, and then looked back at Lisbeth again. She had no time to speak before he went on, "I, er, gave the archbishop reason to believe that you had already accepted me and that I had the blessing of your family. I also, er, gave him reason to believe the matter was urgent."

"Why?" was all that Lisbeth could think to ask.

Apparently cheered by the fact that he had not been thrown out on his ear, Kepley pressed his suit. He came a step closer and would have advanced even more if Miss Winsham had not stopped him with a glare.

"Because my father has procured a special license for me to marry someone else," he explained. "Only I don't wish to marry the lady. But I cannot get my family to listen."

"Why not?" Aunt Margaret asked suspiciously.

Kepley looked at her. "They are very fond of her and have hoped for such a match for some time," he said bluntly. "And I have always refused. So has she. Why she changed her mind, and why it is so urgent to them now, however, I do not know. I only know that unless I marry someone else first, I shall find myself leg-shackled to the lady, and no way out of it."

"That may be, but just what," Miss Winsham asked, fixing the young man with a stern glare, "would my niece gain by marrying you?"

"The freedom granted to a married woman and a handsome allowance to live upon. The expectation, should the fighting be fierce, of being soon rid of the burden of a husband. And if not, well, Miss Barlow is one of the very few females whose company I can abide and I have often thought she felt the same about me."

"You ain't one of those men who prefer men, are you?" Miss Winsham demanded bluntly.

"No, no, upon my hŏnor I am not!" Lord Thomas Kepley made haste to reply, clearly taken aback. He paused, and then said directly to Lisbeth, "You would be a wife—with all the freedom that entails. And I would not be home a great deal to trouble you. You have confided in me your dislike of having to depend upon the kindness of your sisters' husbands. Marry me and you will never need to do so again."

Perhaps it was the plea in his eyes. Perhaps it was the

locket, warm beneath Lisbeth's touch, and the face she thought she had seen when she'd opened it. Perhaps it was all the moments when, as she and Kepley had talked in corners at balls, both feeling like outcasts, she had felt a kindred spirit in his words. Whatever the reason, however foolish it might be, she found herself saying, "Yes."

Within twenty-four hours, Lisbeth found herself wed, within thirty-six she had been bedded, within forty-eight she found herself about to be abandoned as Lord Thomas Kepley left to rejoin Wellington's staff. As he said goodbye to her, Thomas pressed a piece of paper into her hands.

"This is my estate, left to me by an aunt. It is in a state of disrepair, for I am seldom there. But if you do not choose to live with my parents, or do not wish to stay with either of your sisters while I am gone, you may go there and my staff will take good care of you. You may even make whatever repairs or do whatever refurbishing you think best."

There was no time to say more, for Kepley said he must go, that the ship's captain would be eager to catch the next tide. And so, scarcely two days after Lord Thomas Kepley's strange proposal, Lisbeth found herself an abandoned bride, connected to her husband only by the band of gold on her finger and the paper she held in her hand.

After he was gone, she looked again at the paper and saw that her husband had written the names of his solicitor, his banker, as well as the directions to his estate. What on earth, Lisbeth asked herself, had she done?

The Marquess of Aylsham stared at his oldest son, the Earl of Halford. "You must be mistaken! I gave Thomas distinct orders to wed Dalwood's daughter."

"Yes, well, my brother has chosen to marry Lord Henley's youngest daughter instead. And I am not mistaken in the matter, for Thomas came to tell me so himself. He is even now, no doubt, on board ship, headed back to Wellington."

That appeared to render the marquess speechless and Lord Halford pressed the point. "Thomas appeared not to have any notion as to why you wanted him to marry Anna. Why didn't you tell him? Then he might have done as you wished. As it is, you must have known he had too much spirit to submit tamely to your decree."

"Tell him?" the marquess echoed angrily. "Why should I have done so? Good lord, don't you understand that the fewer people who know the truth, the better? Do you really want Thomas to know what you have done? Do you really want him to know that you have betrayed your wedding vows and fathered a child on Lady Anna Dalwood?"

"Better that than to have him marry someone else!" Halford retorted, with just as much heat in his voice. "Now what are we to do? I cannot marry her, nor can James, for we are both already married."

The marquess stared at his eldest son. "I shall take care of the matter," he said.

"How?"

"I don't know, but I shall." The marquess paused, then added grimly, "Bad enough he had to defy me, but one of Henley's daughters? That scapegrace who gambled away his fortune and shot himself, leaving his daughters without a shilling between 'em. Bad blood there. Very bad blood."

"I didn't think you would like that connection," Halford replied. "But what's done is done."

"Not," the marquess said grimly, "if I have anything to say to the matter."

"Don't you understand?" Halford demanded. "Thomas sailed for Portugal, to rejoin Wellington's staff, this afternoon! He is already married to Miss Barlow and worse, he is already gone from London."

"I shall get him back. Get him back and get this marriage annulled," the marquess said with great determination.

"And if you can't?"

"We'll make provisions for the girl. Send her somewhere out of the way to have the child. Arrange another marriage for her."

Halford stared at his father with sheer exasperation. "That might have worked if she was not a Dalwood, Father! But you know as well as I that the daughter of a marquess cannot disappear for some months without a great deal of talk. Nor will her father agree to marriage with just anyone—not without telling him about the child, and I thought that was precisely what we hoped to avoid by having her marry Thomas."

"I will fix this problem!" the marquess repeated. He paused and stared straight into his eldest son's eyes. "Never forget that this is your fault! If you had kept your marriage vows, or at least chosen to dally with a married woman, or even kept a proper mistress, one who would understand these things, there would be no problem to fix!"

Lord Halford went very pale. His eyes fell and he turned and left the room. He could no longer face his father. In the hallway he encountered his other brother, Lord James Kepley.

James grinned at Halford. "Bad mood, is he? I could hear him yelling all the way down to the front hall. I presume you told him about Thomas?"

Halford nodded. "He is not pleased and neither am I."

James cocked his head to the side. "Why not? You, I mean. I can understand that father hates it when anyone disobeys his orders, but why should you care?"

Halford avoided his brother's shrewd eyes. His father was right that the fewer people who knew of his indiscretions, the better. So now he said, with a careless shrug,

"It would have been a far better match than the one Thomas made."

"Do you think so?" James asked, curiosity lively in his voice. "Well, I, for one, am glad Thomas had sufficient spirit to refuse to do father's bidding. I wish you and I had shown similar resolution when it was our turn to marry."

That caused the earl to look at James more closely. "Are you unhappy?" he asked.

Now it was James who shrugged. "I did my duty and married where I was told to marry. As did you. And it has brought cold comfort to us both. At least Thomas chose his own bride, and from what I have heard, she is a gentle, rather taking thing. I, for one, wish him happy."

"Yes, well, Father won't," Halford said grimly. "He'll do his best to cause trouble for the pair of them, mark my words. Indeed, he'll try to have the marriage undone, if he can."

"Well, then," James said lightly, "it's a good thing Thomas has already left for Portugal. There is nothing Father can do now."

Unfortunately, that didn't mean the marquess wouldn't try.

Chapter 2

L ord Thomas Kepley stared at his father. His father
stared back.

"Dead?" Kepley echoed.

"Dead," the Marquess of Aylsham confirmed. "Lady
Anna Dalwood is dead by her own hand. And the child
with her. Before anyone could guess that she was increasing. Which is one small blessing, I suppose. But if
you had done your duty, there would have been no need
for it. She would have been your wife and the child
would have been born a Kepley, as it ought to have
been."

"I might have done so, if you had told me the truth,"
Thomas replied, his voice not altogether steady.

"You ought to have done as I said, simply because I
told you to!" Lord Aylsham thundered.

"You ought to have trusted me enough to explain,"
Thomas countered.

For a long moment the two men stared at each other,
neither giving way an inch. Then, his voice icy with
anger, Thomas said, "Perhaps you ought to save your lec-
tures for my brother, and talk with him about the sanctity
of the marriage vows. If he had not broken them, there
would have been no need for me to marry Lady Anna at
all."

Lord Aylsham slapped his hands flat on the desk.
Slowly he rose to his feet. "I will not have you criticize
your brother," he said, his voice as filled with anger as his

son's. "Halford did his duty. He married where I told him to. He married a woman who does him credit. You married one of Henley's daughters! He was a brute, a coward, and a wastrel! And she, judging by the age of her child, could not keep her wedding vows for even a few weeks after you left. I will never accept her as your wife. So do not speak to me about your brother."

Thomas glared at his father and then turned on his heel and left the room. Indeed, he stopped only to gather his things and bid his mother farewell, though she seemed no more pleased with him than his father had been. And then he left the house. Lord Thomas was going home and it was, he told himself, long overdue.

Lisbeth, Lady Thomas Kepley, pushed her hair back from her forehead. She didn't much feel like a lady, not when she had to pull all the weeds in the garden herself because there were no funds to pay a gardener. Her back ached and her hands hurt and the task was overwhelming. She would never be able to clear away all the weeds to be found in these gardens.

But she would not give up. The same stubbornness that had brought her here to Kepley's estate, determined to manage even without the support that should have been her due as Kepley's wife, kept her at the task of weeding long after another person would have given up.

No, Lisbeth would not let the gardens defeat her, any more than she had let anything else do so. A short distance away, a small child, just learning to walk, tottered on unsteady legs shrieking with glee, away from the woman who was following him, pretending to be a monster in pursuit.

That was another thing, Lisbeth thought. Her son, Tom, ought to have a nursemaid. But there were no funds for that, either. She didn't know what she would have done if Aunt Margaret had not been willing to come live with her here and help with the child.

Just then Tom wobbled over to Lisbeth and she scooped him up. Aunt Margaret smiled as she came over to her niece, but there was a hint of sadness in her voice when she said, "Not what you expected, Elizabeth, is it, when you agreed to marry Kepley? Not what he promised you, either."

Lisbeth tried to smile. "Are you saying it is a fitting judgment on me for wanting an easier life than I had before? For wishing for fine gowns and dinner parties and everything Thomas said I would have?"

Miss Winsham put a hand on her niece's arm. She shook her head and her voice was oddly gentle as she answered. "You wanted what it is natural for a young woman to want. And Lord Thomas seemed a kind and gentle man. I do not wonder that you agreed to marry him."

"Yes, and now I sew for Mrs. Parker the sorts of gowns I once hoped to wear myself," Lisbeth retorted, the bitterness creeping into her voice. "You need not tell me how foolish I was."

"Not so foolish; simply young. And I do not believe you were only thinking of the position you might have when you agreed to marry Kepley," Miss Winsham said. "I remember how you used to look at him. How both of you looked at each other the day you were married. No, you were not foolish at all. Had I been in your shoes I might well have done the same. I simply meant that Kepley ought to have made better provision for you before he left England."

Lisbeth sighed and bit her lower lip. "Thomas did not know that his father would manage to interfere as he did. I am certain that he did not guess his family would be so adamant in refusing to acknowledge our marriage. Nor"—her voice caught on the words—"did he mean to die."

"He said that he might," Miss Winsham reminded her.

"Yes, but those were just words. I knew him well enough to know that it was the last thing he expected. Sometimes I think he believed he would live forever! He certainly didn't expect his ship to sink while sailing to Portugal."

"Well, I still say we ought to visit his parents again," Miss Winsham said stubbornly. "Tom is old enough now that they cannot possibly deny the resemblance."

"They will deny whatever they wish to deny," Lisbeth said wearily, "and well you know it! Come. It is too chilly to linger outside today. Besides, I have work to do, work I promised to have ready for Mrs. Parker by this afternoon. I've yet to finish hemming two of the gowns, and you know that we could use the money."

Lord Thomas Kepley paused in the courtyard of the posting inn. He was almost home and he was very, very tired. All he wanted was to be in his own home, with his own wife. Elizabeth. Just saying her name conjured up for him her restful image—and her kindness.

He didn't care what his father or anyone else might say. Thomas knew that Elizabeth would not have betrayed him. She would not have been unfaithful. He knew that she would have behaved in an honorable way while he was gone. And he hoped that she would welcome him home.

Two hours later, Kepley's carriage drew to a halt in front of his country home. To his weary eyes, it looked in even greater disrepair than he remembered. His batman said nothing, but Thomas knew the fellow well enough to read the unspoken disapproval in George's face.

Reluctantly, Thomas allowed himself to be helped down from the carriage. At times like this, his leg still ached abominably, but his batman knew better than to offer more than a hand to steady him.

Thomas took his time mounting the front steps to the house. Every bit of disrepair seemed like a reproach to him. He ought to have been here, keeping the place in order, not leaving Elizabeth to shoulder the responsibility on her own. But he would make it up to her, he vowed. She would never have to do so again.

The front door opened and Kepley smiled, eager to greet his majordomo. But it wasn't a servant who opened the door—it was Elizabeth.

She stared at him. Her eyes widened. Her voice shook as she said, "Thomas?" Her voice was scarcely a whisper. Then, more loudly, she repeated, "Thomas?"

She flung her arms around him and he embraced her in return, truly feeling as if he had come home, when he held her in his arms like this.

Into his collar she said, all but babbling, "They said you were dead. They told us only a very few of the sailors and none of the passengers escaped drowning. They said you were pulled under the waves. How did you survive? Where have you been all this time?"

Elizabeth stepped back as she asked this last question, and Thomas stared at her face, hungry for the warmth and welcome he saw there. This was what had kept him going. This was what he told himself he would come home to find. This was what he so desperately needed.

And yet, despite his joy at seeing her, Thomas began to be troubled at what he saw. Elizabeth's hair was slipping free of its pins and it looked as though it had not been trimmed in some time. Her gown was not only dirty, as though she had been cleaning or gardening, but it looked as though it had been torn and patched more than a few times.

What the devil was going on? Where was his butler or footman or maid? Why should Elizabeth have answered the door herself—particularly since she had not known it was he who was standing there?

He must have spoken aloud for Elizabeth replied with

some asperity, "I answered the door because there was no one else to do so! Cook is in the kitchen preparing dinner, our one maid is attempting to clean at least part of the house, and Aunt Margaret is bathing your son!"

Thomas gaped at her. Then he drew in a deep breath. "Perhaps," he said with firmness and presence of mind, "we should discuss this inside. It would seem we both have a great deal to tell each other."

Over his shoulder, he said to his batman, who was watching the entire exchange with the greatest fascination, "Just bring the baggage inside, George. Someone will tell you where to put it later."

That drew Elizabeth's attention. "Up the stairs and to the right, the door at the end," she said, directing the fellow to Thomas's old bedroom.

Thomas smiled at the thought of sharing that wonderful room of his with Elizabeth. They would make love in the evening, he told himself, and then they would talk over the events of the day. Perhaps they would even share their hopes and dreams. And in the morning they would wake and rise together to face each new day.

But he was woolgathering. Already his batman was headed up the stairs and Elizabeth was walking toward the study. Thomas followed her, favoring his leg only a little. He was eager to talk with his wife and to catch up with the news of their months apart.

She waited until he was inside the room with her and then firmly closed the door. Elizabeth sat on the edge of a chair and gestured for him to sit in the one that faced hers. She even waited for him to speak first. It was almost, he thought, as though she saw him as a stranger.

Troubled, Thomas tried to tell himself it was understandable. Especially given how long he had been gone, given that she thought he had drowned at sea. Still, he found himself uncertain how to begin. In the end, he began with practical matters.

"Where are the servants, Elizabeth? I used to have a staff of ten in the house alone."

She laughed a bitter laugh. "You could afford to do so," she replied. "I could not. I had no funds to pay for any servants, Thomas. Your cook stayed out of loyalty, and the one housemaid I have, well, she has nowhere else to go."

"But my solicitor and banker—"

"Were persuaded by your father that our marriage may not have been legal. They have allowed me the merest pittance these past two years."

There was even more bitterness in her voice now, and Kepley could not blame her. He was stunned into silence. He knew that his parents had been opposed to the marriage, but he found it hard to believe they would go this far. His father had said nothing of such a step when they spoke in London. But then, to be sure, the marquess had wished mostly to ring a peal over his son's head and tell him how he had failed the family. Thomas had not stayed to hear if his father wished to tell him anything else.

The silence went on too long, but finally he collected his wits sufficiently to say, "There will be no more problems on that score, I promise you! Tomorrow you may send to the village for as many servants as you need. And if you cannot hire enough from there, then we shall send to an agency in London for the rest."

Elizabeth smiled at him, and the lines of worry and fatigue about her eyes seemed to ease just a little. Thomas wanted to draw her into his arms and soothe her and promise her that she need never feel so discouraged again. But something in her manner still held him at arm's length. So he waited.

After a moment, she asked again what she had on the front steps. "Where have you been, Thomas? And why were you reported dead when you were not? Why did you not let anyone know that you were alive?"

He hesitated. A part of him wanted to tell her the truth,

all of it. To confide in Elizabeth now, as he had so often confided in her when they sat and talked at balls in London two years before. But for all that he had failed his father, he had been raised to know his duty and it did not include telling a gently bred lady tales that would give her nightmares. Instead, Thomas settled for part of the truth.

"I did nearly die," he said quietly. "And for a time I scarcely knew who or where I was. Later, well, later it was not possible to come home. Or even to send word that I was alive. I came as soon as I could."

That had the ring of truth and Elizabeth must have heard it in his voice, for now she smiled and said softly, almost shyly, "I am glad to have you home again, Thomas. Come and meet your son."

He nodded, not trusting himself to speak. A son. His son. There were so many days, and even more nights, while he was gone, when he had thought about the son he and Elizabeth might someday have together. And now he did.

She held out her hand to him and he took it. Together they went out of the study and up the stairs to the nursery. Miss Winsham, Elizabeth's aunt, was there with a little boy scarcely old enough to walk. His hair was very fair, more so than Thomas's, just as his own had been as a child, and his eyes were as blue as Thomas knew his own eyes to be.

Kepley took the child and held him. His son. The child looked like him, or so he thought, until he looked at the back of the boy's neck. And then he felt himself go very, very cold. He felt himself instinctively shut into place all the defenses that had always served him so well.

To Elizabeth he said, his voice as cold as the iciness he felt inside, "Your son looks like a very healthy child. You are to be congratulated, madam."

She stared at him, her jaw falling open. She did not

even move to take the child he held out to her. Miss Winsham took the boy instead, her eyes sharp upon his face.

Because he could not stand to look at either his wife or the child, he turned on his heel and left the nursery without another word.

He did not go to his room. Instead, instinctively, Thomas sought out the deserted corridors of the house where once he had found refuge on visits to this house as a child himself. He wanted, he needed, a place where no one would think to look for him—at least not for a little while. Not until he had found a way to recover from the blow he had just been dealt.

Lisbeth watched Thomas go, too stunned to know what to say to stop him. What on earth was wrong? She looked at her aunt.

"What was it about little Tom that upset him?" she asked, bewildered.

"Perhaps he has heard the rumors," Miss Winsham said bluntly. "Perhaps he believes them."

"But he can't!" Lisbeth protested. "He seemed so happy to be home. Surely if he had believed those rumors, he would have said something before I brought him to the nursery. Why would seeing Tom, who looks so very much like he does, change that?"

Miss Winsham looked at the child in her arms. "Yes," she said slowly, "that is precisely the question. What was it he thought he saw or didn't see when he looked at Tom?"

"Does it matter?" Lisbeth asked. "What am I going to do? What are we going to do?"

"You may have to go to Alexandra or Theresa," Miss Winsham replied.

"No! I worked too hard these past twenty months so that they would never have to know how bad things were. I will not impose upon them now. And you are not to tell them, either! You promised, and that promise has not been revoked just because Thomas has returned."

Miss Winsham shook her head. "I was a fool to agree to any sort of secrecy. Why shouldn't your sisters know you need their help?"

"You promised!"

"So I did. And I shall keep my promise, but I shall not like doing so," Miss Winsham warned her. "Perhaps it won't matter. Perhaps Kepley is simply tired and will come to his senses when he has had a chance to rest. What can he do, after all? File a petition for divorce? Neither he nor his family will wish for that kind of scandal."

"What if he refuses to acknowledge Tom as his son?" Lisbeth asked, her face white with fear. "His parents have already done so. Then what? I cannot, I will not, allow Tom to be sent away."

The older woman sighed. "Best not worry about that for now. If it comes to such a threat, we will find a way to deal with it."

Lisbeth looked at Margaret, who still held Tom, and saw the sympathy as well as the worry in her aunt's eyes. She took a deep breath and tried to speak with a cheerfulness she did not truly feel.

"Well, the one thing we may be sure of is that things are about to change," Lisbeth said, trying and failing to keep the worry out of her own voice.

"I wish I could believe it was for better, not worse," Miss Winsham retorted.

"He did say there would be no more worries over money," Lisbeth acknowledged.

Aunt Margaret nodded, but her voice was tart as she said, "Money is not the only consideration that matters, and well you know it! You will have a difficult time ahead if he means to persist in his foolishness." She paused, then frowned. "What are you going to do about Mrs. Parker? I cannot think Kepley will wish you to continue. Do you even mean to tell him about the sewing you have been doing for her? That it was how you have earned the money to put food on the table?"

Lisbeth gave a gasp. "I'd forgotten about Mrs. Parker! I'd best send word to her in the village that I cannot see her today, after all. Perhaps she can come tomorrow morning, before Thomas is awake."

"You are too late," Miss Winsham said, glancing out the window. "I see her coming up the back path right now. You had best explain to her the change in your circumstances without delay."

Without a word, Lisbeth turned and ran from the room. She had to see Mrs. Parker and warn her. The Marquess of Aylsham, when he denounced her marriage to Thomas, had talked to her of consequence and breeding and what was due the family name. He would not have been pleased to learn of the sewing Lisbeth did for Mrs. Parker, and she very much feared that Thomas might not like it, either. Matters were strained enough between them already, though taking in sewing for money was a small matter beside the fact that he thought Tom was not his son. How on earth was she ever going to change his mind?

Miss Winsham watched her niece go and worried. She wished she had never given Elizabeth the locket—or at least not until after Kepley had left England twenty months ago, at any rate. She had been foolish, Margaret told herself, to believe in the nonsensical legend. And yet, a tiny part of her hoped that Lord Thomas was the man Elizabeth was meant to marry, that in the end he would make her happy.

With a sigh, Miss Winsham settled Tom onto his cot and read him a story. With luck, he would nap, and with luck, Kepley would come to his senses.

Chapter 3

L ord Thomas wandered the halls of the house that had been his since he inherited the estate at the age of twenty-one. The house was in need of repairs, but so far as he could tell, Elizabeth had not changed anything while he was gone. And yet it did not feel the same. It felt like a stranger's house. But perhaps that was because he was the stranger here—even to himself.

He tried to find some sense of calm, some hope for himself and Elizabeth. Once he would have sworn she could never, would never, be unfaithful to him. But he had been mistaken. And short of the scandal of divorce, Thomas thought bitterly, they were bound to each other for the rest of their lives.

He took a deep breath and tried to tell himself that perhaps she had reason to seek comfort elsewhere. He had, after all, pushed her into marriage with himself for selfish reasons, without giving her a chance to consider the matter thoroughly. What right had he to be angry with her for anything?

Elizabeth had come to him untouched, Thomas reminded himself. And if another man had fathered her child, surely it was after she thought he was dead. Surely there could be no point in blaming her for what she could not have known was a betrayal.

Nor could Thomas see blaming the child. He knew only too well what it was like to have a father who found him an unsatisfactory son. He could not do the same thing to this innocent.

It was just, he thought with a sigh, that he wished Elizabeth had the courage to tell him the truth. He didn't want to have to tell her why he was so certain the child could not be his. He wanted, instead, for her to tell him the truth because she trusted him enough to do so.

No one else, in his life, other than his fellow military officers, had ever believed in Lord Thomas Kepley. He had been a disappointment to his parents from the day he was born. His brothers had been older and all but shut him out of their lives. The *ton* thought him a heedless scapegrace. But Miss Elizabeth Barlow had once believed in him. And now, he wished desperately that she would believe in him again.

Because his thoughts were intolerable to him, Thomas looked out the window at the end of the hallway. He saw a woman coming up toward the back of the house. It looked like one of the women from the village. Did Elizabeth perhaps hire someone to help with the meals, he wondered?

Suddenly he found it important to know just how his wife had managed while he was gone. Thomas decided to go downstairs and speak to the woman. If she was someone Elizabeth had hired from the village, perhaps he could ask her to take word back that, starting tomorrow, he wished to hire a number of servants to work in the house.

It took him some time, but eventually he found Elizabeth and the woman in one of the small parlors at the back of the house. To his astonishment, he found the two women surrounded by fabric and partially made dresses.

Startled, Thomas paused in the doorway, but he must have made some sort of sound for both women immediately looked toward him. Was that guilt he saw upon their faces?

"M-my lord," the woman said.

"Thomas!" Elizabeth exclaimed. "I, that is, didn't you wish to rest? Or perhaps tour the estate, now that you are back?"

Puzzled, he came forward into the room, carefully closing the door behind him. In something of a drawl he said, "It would seem you are wasting no time adjusting to your changed circumstances, madam. Just how many"— he paused to survey the quantity of fabric and half-made dresses before he went on—"gowns do you plan to purchase?"

And why that question should throw Elizabeth into confusion was beyond him. But both women looked at each other, the hint of guilt more pronounced than ever.

"I, er, that is to say, I don't know. Mrs. Parker brought everything she had, so as to see what would suit me," Elizabeth replied.

Thomas started to nod, but caught himself as he remembered what he had seen from his window. In the same drawl as before he said, "How very odd. I could have sworn that when I saw Mrs. Parker approaching the house from the rear she was carrying nothing at all."

"I, er, sent this up, in me son's wagon," Mrs. Parker answered hastily. "I'd heard you was back and bethought me that the mistress would be wanting something pretty to wear for you. P'rhaps even lots of somethings pretty."

"You must have seen my carriage pass by the village," Thomas said, "and wasted no time coming here." To Elizabeth, he added, "You were so sure, then, that I would approve of such extravagance?"

Elizabeth blushed. She looked at Mrs. Parker. She looked back at him. "I, that is, I was just explaining to Mrs. Parker that she was mistaken and would need to take everything home with her."

Mrs. Parker made a sound of dismay. It did not surprise Thomas in the least that the seamstress was dis-

tressed to hear the dashing of her hopes for a generous
sale. And all at once he was tired of taunting them.

"No, no," he said, waving a hand carelessly. "Choose
as many gowns as you like. It is past time you were properly dressed, and now that I am home you may do so."

The two women looked at each other, not nearly as
delighted as he would have expected. It was Elizabeth
who said, at last, "I, er, thought perhaps Mrs. Parker
could leave this with me for a day or two while I decide?"

Thomas would have expected the seamstress to object, but she nodded her head vigorously. Well, perhaps
she expected a very large sale to come of this. It was no
matter to him, for he could well afford to indulge Elizabeth. So he shrugged and said, "As you wish. I shall
leave you to settle the matter between you. Good-day,
Mrs. Parker."

He paused and then turned back to them, catching yet
another odd look as it passed between the pair. He
frowned but merely said, "Oh, by the by, when do you
serve dinner in this house?"

Elizabeth looked at Mrs. Parker, then back at Thomas.
Her voice was not altogether steady as she replied, "I . . .
that is . . . We have become accustomed, Aunt Margaret
and I, to eating in the kitchen with Tom at a very early
hour. There are no servants to serve the food in the dining room or, even if we served ourselves, to watch him
while we eat there."

For a very long moment, he stared at her, still trying to
grasp the extent of the circumstances she had coped with
for the past twenty months. She held her breath, as
though afraid of what he might say, and abruptly Thomas
felt ashamed.

"Tomorrow," he said, with what he hoped was a reassuring smile, "all of that changes. We hire servants from
the village. I will not have my wife acting the part of a
drudge! There is gossip enough without that. No, nor any

further need for it. Now that I am back, there will be an end to all that. For tonight, have a tray sent up to my room. I am tired and I wish to rest."

And then Thomas left the parlor. He went back upstairs to see if his batman had finished unpacking his belongings. It still felt strange to him to have a servant to do such things for him. For twenty months he had managed on his own. To be sure, he had not been moving in social circles and it had scarcely mattered. But now it did.

Still, Thomas had been glad to find his old batman willing to return to his service and far preferred him to the fashionable valet his father had wished him to hire instead. He wondered if George had found out anything about the household yet. It was, he recalled, one of the chief advantages of having a servant loyal to one's person. One often found out, through the fellow, things no one wished to say to him. If there were secrets here, odds were that George would find them out before he did.

Lisbeth and Mrs. Parker looked at each other and let out the breaths they had been holding.

"What are we going to do?" the seamstress asked.

Lisbeth did not hesitate. "You will take the finished gowns with you today. All but one, at any rate. If I keep none of them, he will wonder. I'll do as much as I can over the next couple of days to finish these others."

"And after that?" Mrs. Parker demanded. "I've orders that must be filled!"

"I think," Lisbeth said, "you had best start looking for someone else who can sew."

The seamstress started to argue but stopped herself and nodded. "Aye," she said begrudgingly. "If he don't want his wife acting the part of a drudge, it's not likely he'll be happy to find out you've been sewing for me, either. Ah, well, you was the handiest with a needle I've ever met, and I've been lucky to have you as long as I did."

Lisbeth helped Mrs. Parker wrap up the finished gowns in muslin and walked her to the back door. Then she went in search of Cook to see if something special could be arranged for dinner.

George, Kepley's batman, had already unpacked and disappeared. Thomas thought about going in search of him, but decided that it didn't matter. George would no doubt reappear later in the afternoon. Thomas tried to focus his mind on the house and the estate, and what repairs would need to be done. But instead his treacherous thoughts kept returning to Elizabeth.

There was not a trace of her in the room. Evidently she had not used it while he was gone. Was it because she could not bear the thought of sleeping here without him? Or because she would have felt too guilty, once she had been unfaithful? And would she join him in this room, now that he was back?

He remembered how adamant Elizabeth had once been about clinging to spinsterhood—until he'd changed her mind. He remembered, as if it were yesterday, the look in her eyes when he did, the sweet smile with which she had said her wedding vows.

It was very hard to reconcile the tired woman who had greeted him at the door and now looked at him with such weariness in her eyes, with the laughing creature he had held in his arms when they'd made love the one night they'd had together after they were married.

Even as Thomas thought these words, the images came vividly back to him. As if it were yesterday, he could remember the sight of Elizabeth's long light brown hair flowing free about her shoulders. As if it were yesterday, he could recall the soft scent of lilac that she wore and the feel of her skin beneath his hands.

He remembered only too well the shy wonder in her eyes as she discovered how wonderful it could be between a woman and a man. And it was as if he could still hear her startled cry as she flew over the edge to completion with him.

Did she remember? he wondered. And if she did, was it with joy or trepidation?

Thomas scarcely knew or cared how long he stood there. He only knew that he could not let go of the memories. Nor did he want to let go of them. Those memories were what had sustained him for the last twenty months. These memories were also, if he were honest enough to admit it, what scared the devil out of, or rather, into him.

And he did not know how to reconcile those memories with the knowledge that Elizabeth must have been unfaithful. As hard as it was to believe, the proof was in the child. For all her claims that he was the father, Thomas knew that to be impossible.

As he stood there, lost in thought, there came an odd tapping at the door. He opened it to find Elizabeth standing there holding a tray with both her hands and about to tap the door again, with her foot, which accounted for the oddness of the sound.

She flushed under his scrutiny. "I have not learned how to balance a tray with one hand and knock with the other," she said.

Thomas frowned. "Why are you bringing up my tray yourself?" he demanded. "I told you to send it up with the maid."

Again her chin came up, and she moved into the room and waited for the door to close behind her before she answered him. "She is busy with other things," Elizabeth said.

"You could have had my man bring it up."

She drew in a breath, as though trying to draw in courage as well. "I thought," she said, "that perhaps this

would be a chance for us to talk, to begin to become reacquainted with each other."

For a moment, Thomas felt his heart leap with hope,
but then he realized that Elizabeth's thoughts were not
likely to be the same as his had been right before she
knocked. Still, she had taken the time to change her gown
and rearrange her hair. He took that as a promising sign.

"I see," he told her gravely. "Of course. How wise. But
what about your son? Who is taking care of him?"

There was a flash of anger in her eyes. "Aunt Margaret
is with *our* son," she said, her voice daring him to contradict her choice of words.

He did not. "I see," he merely said.

Then, to cover his confusion, Thomas went over to the
table where she had set down the tray of food and noted
with approval that she had brought enough for two. At his
gesture, she sat near him and let him serve her first.

"What," he asked when they began to eat, "do you
suggest we talk about?"

"Whatever you wish."

Somehow he did not think that quite the truth, but he
let it pass. "What happened?" he asked quietly. "How did
things come to such a pass? I certainly meant to leave you
sufficient funds to live better than this."

Elizabeth closed her eyes and drew in a deep breath;
then she met his gaze squarely. There was hurt and anger
but strength as well, both in her eyes and in her voice,
when she replied.

"Your father would not accept our marriage," she said.
"He accused me of somehow entrapping you and threatened to have it annulled. He refused to acknowledge me,
and so neither did the *ton.*"

She paused and took another breath, then forced herself to go on. "That was hard enough, but after we heard
you had been drowned at sea, and I realized that I might
be carrying our child, I went to see Lord Aylsham one
more time. I took the marriage lines with me, to show

him. Foolishly, I thought the sight of them would change his mind. But when I handed the marriage lines over for him to look at, he tore them up. He swore I should not profit a cent from the marriage. And when I told him again that I was carrying your child, he called me a liar. He called me worse, as well. He refused to believe you could have sired a child before you left."

"Conceived in that one night, I suppose?" Thomas could not help but ask.

She heard the sarcasm in his voice and she flushed. But Elizabeth continued to meet his eyes steadily with her own. And her voice was also steady as she replied, "Yes, he was conceived in that one night."

"Tell me the truth," Thomas said gently. "I promise I shall understand and not blame you. I know that you were alone and perhaps you were frightened. I married you in haste, then promptly disappeared. You thought I was dead. I would not blame you, indeed I do not blame you, whatever the truth might be."

"I have told you the truth!" she said, meeting his eyes with her own stormy gaze, not troubling to hide her anger. "Tom is your son, whether you wish to believe it or not!"

He looked at her and knew it was useless to try to tell her again that she need not be afraid to tell him the truth. That he would forgive her if she did. She was determined to persist in saying it was his child. Thomas almost wished it were true. He would have liked to be a father. But he had seen the child, examined the child, and it was impossible.

How ironic, he thought. He had refused to marry one woman, not knowing she carried a Kepley child, and now he found himself married to a woman who had born a son who was not a Kepley. It was no wonder that his father was furious with him. He had incurred scandal for himself and for his family with nothing to show for it but this.

Almost imperceptibly, he withdrew, though he was

scarcely aware of doing so. He became Lord Thomas Kepley, remote and aloof, as so many people perceived him to be. And yet he tried. He reached out and took Elizabeth's hand in his.

"We need to get to know each other again," he told her quietly. "We need to show the world my father is—and has been—wrong to deny you as my wife."

For a moment, Thomas thought she would snatch her hand away, but she did not, even though it trembled in his. Her chin came up, in the same gesture of unconscious defiance as before, and he was glad to see a trace of the spirit he had once so admired.

"Very well," she said.

"We were friends once," Thomas added, almost coaxingly. "Or, at least I thought we were. I should like for us to be friends again. It would be a start."

She nodded. "It would," she acknowledged.

Thomas waited, but she said nothing more and he sighed inwardly. It was a start. But it was also less, far less, than he had hoped for. He could scarcely blame Elizabeth, and yet part of him was also impatient with her. Had she forgotten, he wondered, that night they had shared, twenty months ago? Would she ever want another like it?

As if she could read his mind, Elizabeth spoke, her voice trembling almost as much as her hand. "I will not deny you your rights as my husband, if that is what you were asking."

Had there been one spark of desire for him to be seen in her eyes, Thomas would have drawn her into his arms, then and there, and kissed her until she remembered what he remembered. But he saw only what looked like a mixture of fear and determination in her expression.

He touched her cheek and she smiled, albeit nervously. Thomas sighed. "I will not have a bloodless marriage," he told her, meeting her gaze squarely and letting her see that he meant what he said. "We will share a bed again.

But not tonight, for I do not think that you are ready for that yet. And perhaps neither am I."

How he wished her relief were not so evident! How he wished there had been at least a trace of disappointment or regret in her eyes!

Abruptly, Thomas let go of Elizabeth's hand. He rose to his feet and went to stand by the window, as though fascinated by the view. Over his shoulder, he said, "Send for servants tomorrow. And it is just as well you asked that dressmaker here today. You are very much in need of decent clothing. I will not have my wife looking so bedraggled."

Silence. He waited, but she did not speak, and some perverse devil made him add, "Or perhaps it would be best to order just one or two gowns here and then, once we get to London, replenish your entire wardrobe with everything you need."

"We . . . We are going to London?"

He heard the fear in her voice and he turned to face her. He kept his hands clasped tightly behind him so that he would not reach out to touch or hold her.

"Yes. I have heard the rumors, you see. There is only one way to put paid to them, and that is for us to be seen together on patently friendly terms. I must be seen to dote on my wife—and upon my son."

"When?"

"I have not yet decided."

"But why?" Elizabeth asked, bewildered. "I can see that you do not believe he is your son."

She had not meant to speak aloud, or so Thomas guessed, for the moment the words were spoken, she looked as if she wished she could take them back.

Thomas sighed again. He went over to Elizabeth and drew her into his arms. She did not fight him, and he let himself hold her close for a moment, breathing in the scent of her hair. He kissed the top of her head.

In a voice that betrayed how tightly his emotions were

held in check, he said, "I will not have my name, or yours, bandied about, Elizabeth. I will not have your son's paternity the subject of endless gossip. What is done is done, and we must and we shall make the best of it."

And then, because he could not hold her much longer and still keep his desire in check, Thomas let go of Elizabeth and pushed her away. "You had better go and see to your son," he said.

She turned then, and fled the room. In the silence left behind, Thomas clenched his hands into fists. What the devil had he just done? Elizabeth was his wife and he had just driven her away.

But he had also told her that they would share a bed. He meant it, too. But not just yet, not when she was so afraid and he was so angry. He wanted Elizabeth to come willingly to him. Tomorrow he would begin his campaign to wear down her defenses.

But for tonight it was his own heart with which he had to wrestle. For all his words to the contrary, for all that his mind knew he should not blame Elizabeth for seeking comfort when she thought he was dead, deep in his heart, Thomas did so. And he did not know if he could ever let his anger go.

She would not be afraid, Lisbeth told herself. Thomas was her husband and she would keep the bargain she had made. She had too much honor to do anything else.

Still, it hurt that he did not believe her. And when she looked at him now, he seemed such a stranger to her! Where was the man who had once laughed with her, held her, and treated her with such kindness? It would be a relief, to be sure, to have no more worries about how to pay the bills, but Lisbeth would have traded prosperity for a glimpse of the man she had once thought she might someday be able to love.

Another thought assailed her. Lisbeth had been accustomed to running her own household for almost two years now. It would not be easy to hand the reins back over to a husband. And he would expect her to do so. She knew that he would, even though the words had not yet been spoken. No longer would she be able to think only of her own and Tom's and Aunt Margaret's wishes. Now she would be expected to adapt herself to Lord Thomas Kepley's wishes as well, and Lisbeth was not at all certain that she could.

She had an even darker thought, one to match the growing darkness outside. What if Thomas turned out to be like her father? When they were in London, she had learned, her father could appear charming and kind—just as Thomas had. It was an image that had been difficult for her to reconcile with the tyrant who had ruled their home with never a thought for their mother's feelings or those of his children. Was Thomas such a mixture of contradictions?

Lisbeth knew she was very selfish to think of it, but she almost wished Thomas had not returned. But he had, and now she had to deal with the reality. It would not be easy for her. She had never been a meek and biddable creature.

There was a rap at the door and then it opened. Aunt Margaret, come to say good night. All these months they had grown accustomed to retiring early, with the sunset almost, because candles were so dear. That, too, no doubt would change. But for now, Lisbeth welcomed the familiar ritual.

Miss Winsham hugged her niece and looked into her eyes with as piercing a gaze as Thomas had used a short time earlier—and with equally perspicacious results.

"That bad, was it?" Miss Winsham asked grimly. "Shall we pack our things and run away?"

Lisbeth shook her head. "There is nowhere to go. Besides, I made a bargain with Thomas, when I agreed to marry him. I will not renege on it now. He is a good man,

I think, and already he has told me to hire all the servants
we need. And to purchase myself new gowns."

"I see," Aunt Margaret said, and Lisbeth feared she
did. Then the older woman added shrewdly, "But he still
does not believe the child is his?"

Lisbeth shook her head, not trusting herself to speak.
Margaret snorted. "Men! All alike, the fools! Well, if you
are determined to stay, then so shall I. Tom is tucked into
bed and the maid laid down in her usual cot beside him.
But he is asking for you."

Lisbeth nodded. "I shall go to him at once."

Miss Winsham stepped aside to let her niece pass, but
at the last moment she stopped her with a light touch on
her arm. "Give yourself time," she said. "And him. If you
are determined to keep your bargain, then truly keep it.
Give yourselves both a chance to discover how you may
do so and be happy."

Again Lisbeth could only nod. Aunt Margaret let go of
her sleeve and Lisbeth moved down the hallway as
swiftly as she could to the nursery. There she stopped on
the threshold, for Kepley stood staring down at his son,
uncertainty clearly writ upon his face.

For a moment, Lisbeth feared what he meant to do;
then her breath came in a soft sigh of relief as she saw the
gentleness with which he touched his son's cheek. He did
not believe her; she knew that all too well. It broke her
heart, but truly she understood.

What man would not have doubted, returning under
the circumstances that he did? The true measure of his
character was that even disbelieving her words, Thomas
did not mean to turn her out. Nor, it seemed, did he mean
to take out his disbelief and anger on the child. For that,
Lisbeth would always be grateful. For that, she would
forgive him almost anything.

Quietly she moved to stand beside Kepley and even
slip an arm about his waist. He started at that, but did not

object, not even when she rested her head against his shoulder.

At the sight of her face, Tom smiled and lay quiet, knowing she would sing to him. And she did, though it meant moving away from Kepley and closer to his son. For some time, Thomas stayed and listened. It was only when she was done, and Tom was asleep, that Lisbeth realized her husband had disappeared.

Chapter 4

By the time Thomas came downstairs the next morning Lisbeth had already sent to the village for more servants, and several new maids were busy giving the house the cleaning it so badly needed.

In addition, a good breakfast had been laid out in the dining room in anticipation of whenever Thomas should choose to rise and come downstairs in search of sustenance. Lisbeth made certain the new servants would warn her the moment he showed signs of being awake. Thus it was that when Thomas entered the dining room, he found Lisbeth and Miss Winsham calmly eating breakfast.

He checked himself in the doorway and there was no mistaking his surprise. But he recovered quickly and came forward to greet them. "Good morning Elizabeth, Miss Winsham."

Thomas allowed himself to be served by one of the newly hired servants, then nodded to Lisbeth. "You have been busy," he said with what she took to be approval.

"I rose at dawn," she replied. "There seemed no reason to delay carrying out your wishes."

He nodded again. "The child?" he asked.

"With the nursemaid I hired. She is an older woman who is accustomed to looking after children."

Thomas hesitated. "I am surprised," he said cautiously, "that you were able to find so many servants so quickly in such a small village. I thought we would have to send to London for some."

Lisbeth answered with equal care. "We shall. But apparently many of the servants worked here before and they were happy to do so again. It is, at the very least, a start. Certainly a luxury compared to the circumstances to which we accustomed ourselves these past months."

She held her breath, wanting to hear that Thomas was pleased, wanting to hear that he valued what she had done. And perhaps he was pleased, for some of the rigidness seemed to go out of the way he sat. She didn't quite know, Lisbeth thought, how to deal with this man who was both her husband and at the same time almost a stranger.

Just as she was starting to relax, he turned his attention to Aunt Margaret. "I thank you, Miss Winsham, for being such a help to my wife while I was gone," he said.

"You are very welcome. And are you perhaps trying to tell me that my services are no longer needed?" Aunt Margaret asked bluntly.

He looked taken aback. There was also a hint of guilt in his eyes. If he had meant that, Lisbeth thought, he was too polite to say so. Instead, he smiled, albeit briefly.

"I? Wish to send away someone who can help to work miracles?" Thomas countered. "I should think not!"

They stared, each taking the measure of the other. Both seemed, for the moment at any rate, satisfied with what they found.

The peaceful tableau was shattered a moment later, however, when a footman appeared in the doorway, out of breath. To Lisbeth he said, "Ma'am, the child—he's ill! You're asked to come at once!"

Lisbeth did not hesitate. She did not stop to look if Margaret were following, for she knew that as a matter of course, her aunt would do so.

Upstairs, in the nursery, Thomas watched from the doorway as Elizabeth, her aunt, and a female servant clustered around the boy. His breathing seemed alarmingly loud, and despite his determination to keep aloof from the boy, Thomas found himself turning and speaking to the footman who had summoned them from the breakfast room.

"Send someone for the nearest physician," Thomas said. "Tell him the matter is urgent."

The fellow nodded and sped down the stairs driven as much, perhaps, by the sounds the poor child was making as by the orders he had been given or the coin Lord Thomas had slipped into his hand.

In the nursery, Miss Winsham was boiling a pot of water in the nursery fireplace. She was tossing in what looked like a handful of herbs even as Elizabeth and the nursery maid created some sort of tent nearby. Clearly this was something Elizabeth and her aunt had done often, and when the nursery maid protested, Elizabeth took the child herself, ducked into the tent, and sat on the floor inside it holding her son.

A moment later, Miss Winsham set the pot of boiling water inside the tent with mother and child, closed the blanket around them, and then straightened and glared at the nursery maid.

"If you wish to keep your post," she told the poor woman, "you will do as you are told! If you listen, you will hear that the boy's breathing is already easier. His mother and I know what we are about. A tent with a pot of boiling water will do wonders. And when it cools, the tea I have brewed in that pot will help the child's breathing even more."

The nursery maid muttered something, and to Kepley it sounded like the word "witchcraft." Miss Winsham snorted.

"Anyone who bothered to study plants would know what to do," she said "It takes no witchcraft, only the use of one's wits and a willingness to learn from others. Now, fetch me a mug so that I may pour some of that tea into it to cool."

The nursery maid did as she was bid and did not try to interfere. Indeed, as the child's breathing eased, so did the rigidity of the nursery maid's stance. Her voice may have seemed reluctant, but her words offered a truce as she said to Miss Winsham, "It might be a good notion if you showed me how to brew that tea."

Miss Winsham nodded and proceeded to oblige. Thomas could not explain the relief he felt. Why should he care whether the nursery staff and Miss Winsham got along? Why should he worry so much over a child he had never seen until yesterday?

But he did worry; he did care. It was an unsettling notion, for over the past twenty months, Thomas had done his best to learn how not to care. Indeed, he had done his best not to feel anything—except the need to do his work and survive. And yet, despite all his practice, he found he could not help but care about the child in the tent.

He turned to go, hoping to slip away before anyone noticed he had even been there. But Miss Winsham caught his eye. "I will wish to speak with you shortly, sir," she said.

He bowed. "I shall be in the breakfast room when you are ready."

She nodded curtly and he was taken aback by her rudeness until he realized that all her thoughts, all her concern, must be taken up by the child. She had neither time nor energy for courtesy, and in her shoes, Thomas admitted sourly, he would very likely have been the same.

In the end, it was quite some time before Miss Winsham went in search of him. And she found Kepley not in the breakfast room but in a small study set aside for handling the estate accounts. Thomas was attempting to ascertain what had been done on the estate in his absence.

True to what he remembered of her, Miss Winsham marched into the room, and without waiting for him to acknowledge her, she began to speak. "Was it you who sent for the physician?" she demanded. "Must have been, I suppose. Haven't met him before, but he seems to know what he is about. At any rate, he's better than most of his ilk. He knew enough not to bleed the boy or otherwise subject him to the sorts of cruel handling most of them seem to delight in! But then, he is university educated, and I suppose that makes a difference."

When Miss Winsham paused for breath, Thomas ruthlessly cut her short. "How is the child?" he demanded. When she hesitated he added sharply, "Come, come—I'll have the truth, if you please."

"Your son," she replied, emphasizing those two words with grim determination, "and he *is* your son, suffers from difficulty breathing, particularly if he is distressed or overexerts himself in some way."

"I see. And what does the doctor say?"

"The doctor says"—an older gentleman answered from the doorway of the book room—"that idle ladies ought not to fancy themselves physicians! Nor quack their children or niece's children with nonsensical remedies they have culled from recipe books of their mothers and grandmothers."

Miss Winsham seethed with rage. Thomas had never seen her in a temper before, but there was no mistaking how she felt now. She advanced upon the doctor and Thomas had the oddest feeling he ought to throw himself between the pair. Instead, he merely watched.

"Oh?" Miss Winsham asked in a deceptively mild voice. "You think so, do you, Dr. Brooks? Well, I think that physicians, university educated or not, ought not to dismiss a treatment merely because it is something they do not understand!"

"Madam, you are speaking nonsense!"

"Am I? Then why did my methods bring the child ease? What do you have to offer that would have served him as well or better?"

"Mere coincidence!"

"Every time?" Miss Winsham demanded.

The doctor began to splutter. Finally he drew himself up to his full height and said, with great precision, "I have only your word for that."

"Then stay! Once he begins to have such attacks, they generally go on for days. Stay and I can promise you a chance to observe firsthand what that child endures. And you may satisfy yourself as to whether my methods help or do harm."

"I cannot stay," Dr. Brooks protested. "My other patients might have need of me."

"Send a note to your housekeeper to send for you here, if you are needed," Miss Winsham replied. "I am certain Lord Thomas will not mind doing so for you. Of course, if you fear discovering that you are wrong . . ."

She allowed her voice to trail off neatly. Kepley watched as the doctor's eyes narrowed and he took the bait. "Very well," the fellow said with great dignity and disdain, "I shall stay. That is, if you are willing, sir, to have me."

He asked this of Thomas, who promptly bowed his assent. The physician permitted himself a small smile. "One must deal with quackery wherever one finds it," he added. "May I borrow pen, ink, and paper? And will you be so good as to have my message delivered to my housekeeper?"

"Certainly," Thomas agreed, not troubling to hide his amusement. "You may use this desk, if you wish. I shall go let my wife know that you will be staying with us for a few days."

"I shall tell Elizabeth!" Miss Winsham said quickly. "Dr. Brooks, I shall see you later."

And then she was gone. The two men looked at each other. Thomas gestured to the desk. "You will find everything you need to write your letter in here," he said.

The physician nodded. "Thank you," he said. "It cannot be comfortable for you," he added with a grimace as he sat down at the desk to write his note, "having such a termagant in your household."

Thomas hesitated. "I don't know yet," he admitted. "I have only been home one day, and thus far Miss Winsham's ire has not been directed at me."

"It will be," Dr. Brooks predicted gloomily. "It will be. That sort of female can never resist interfering where she does not belong."

Thomas chose not to argue. What did it matter, anyway, his opinion or the doctor's? Either Miss Winsham would interfere or she would not, and no amount of words between himself and the physician would affect the truth one jot.

Apparently Dr. Brooks took his silence for assent, for he turned his attention entirely upon the letter he wished to write. After he was done, however, and the message folded and ready to be handed over to a footman, the physician must have looked more closely at Thomas.

"You don't look well," Brooks said bluntly. "Prisoner of war?"

Startled, Thomas looked at the physician. The other man nodded. "Thought so. Been called in to treat a few. Nerves, mostly. Can't have been pleasant for you fellows."

Torn between amusement and annoyance at the other man's impertinence, Thomas said, "You merely think this? Didn't any of them tell you whether it was or not?"

Dr. Brooks frowned. "Devilish unwilling to talk about any of it—as you seem to be as well. Don't suppose you'll confide in me, either." Thomas shook his head and the physician went on. "Do you a world of good if you did confide in someone. If not in me, then your wife."

"No!"

One word, spoken sharply, curtly, answered the doctor. He didn't bother to argue. He was obviously not the sort of man to waste his time on futile endeavors.

As the silence stretched on, and Thomas realized that

Dr. Brooks did not mean to persist, he began to relax a trifle. He even unbent sufficiently to offer the physician whiskey or brandy. The other man shook his head.

"Oh, no. I mean to keep my wits completely clear. Miss Winsham is not going to get the better of me because I got myself befuddled with drink!" Dr. Brooks said.

Thomas refrained from pointing out that one drink was scarcely likely to have so profound an impact upon the man. It was, after all, possible that Dr. Brooks was one of those few unfortunates who could not drink at all without succumbing to intoxication. So he settled for offering the physician the run of his house and grounds instead.

"Would you mind if I looked over your library?" Dr. Brooks asked, his expression brightening at the thought. "I looked in there, while trying to find you, and noticed that you seem to have a very fine collection of scientific texts."

"Of course. I should be very happy to have you do so," Thomas replied, relieved at the notion of having the physician, with his far too shrewd eyes, anywhere save in the same room with him.

Ten minutes later, Thomas was going over the estate accounts again in splendid peace and silence.

Chapter 5

Lisbeth watched her son sleep. She held on tight to the locket at her throat for comfort. It seemed cold to the touch, and she wondered whether to curse it or thank it for her marriage to Thomas. Right now, she could not see how things would ever be right between them. And yet, if she had not seen the face in the locket, if she had not married Kepley, she would not have her son, Tom, either.

He stirred in his sleep and coughed, and she held her breath until he stopped. Were the attacks getting worse? If so, what were she and Aunt Margaret to do? Dr. Brooks was not as bad as some had been, but he did not seem to have answers either. What if no one did?

It was a fear that had haunted Lisbeth for far too long. And now it was made worse by the grim expression she had seen on Thomas's face earlier. Would he come to see Tom as an increasing nuisance if the attacks continued or grew worse? Particularly if he continued to refuse to believe the child was his son?

Perhaps when they went to London she could find a better physician. But Lisbeth had already tried writing the best of them for advice for her son and they had written back that there was nothing to be done. Lisbeth refused to believe them. This was her son and she would care for him, with Aunt Margaret's help, no matter what anyone else told her.

The sweet sound of soft, easy breathing came now

from the bed and Lisbeth allowed herself to close her eyes. Just for a moment, she thought.

Some time later, Lisbeth became aware of voices intruding into her dreams. Not just voices, but voices shouting. If she could hear it all the way in the nursery, it must be very, very loud. Instantly Lisbeth found herself awake and on her feet headed downstairs. Whatever the trouble was, she'd best take a hand in resolving it.

Lisbeth had no trouble finding the source of the shouting. Indeed, had her own ears not been sufficient to direct her, the cluster of servants in the hallway outside the drawing room would have informed her of where the sounds were coming from. At the sight of Lady Thomas, the servants scattered, and after taking a deep breath, Lisbeth opened the door and stepped inside.

She was not entirely pleased to see Lord Peter Dalwood there. He had made a number of attempts, over the past year and a half or so, to establish a friendship between them. But something about him made her uneasy and she had always kept him at arm's length. But now he did not behave as if she had.

Dalwood bowed and came toward Lisbeth. He took her hands and lifted them to his lips and kissed each one before she could snatch them away. There was, or so it seemed, great concern in his voice as he said, "My poor, dear girl! You look all done up."

"My son is sick again," she said, taking a step back, trying to put some distance between them.

Dalwood took another step toward her. From behind him, Lisbeth heard Thomas's voice. It was rough with a number of emotions, including anger, as he said, "Dalwood is right, Elizabeth, you are all done up. Go upstairs and rest. I am certain *our* guest will understand."

The stress on the word "our" was slight but unmistakable. Was Thomas jealous that Dalwood had come to call? Was that why he was so angry? Was he perhaps worried about her reputation? Or was he worried about his own?

Lisbeth was too tired to sort it out. She looked at Dalwood. "My husband is right. I do need to go back upstairs to my son."

Before she could stop him, Lord Peter reached out and took her hands in his once again. He gave all the appearance of an old friend who was accustomed to run tame in the house—and with her.

"I will not trouble you with my presence then," Dalwood said, his voice full of warmth. "Your thoughts can only have one direction at such a time. How fortunate your husband is here at your side, to be a support to you."

Lisbeth turned and fled the room. Behind her, she could hear the conversation resume between Dalwood and her husband and the tone was not a friendly one. Outside the room, she hesitated. It wasn't proper, but she could not resist the opportunity to discover the source of the animosity between Lord Peter and Thomas.

Inside the drawing room, the two men stared at each other. "Only fitting, don't you think," Dalwood said with a smile that held no friendship, "that since you ruined my sister, I should have a shot at your wife? We have become friends while you were gone. Extremely good friends."

Thomas controlled himself only with the greatest effort. A brawl between himself and Dalwood would only seem to confirm the gossip he wished so dearly to confound. Aloud he said, "I did not ruin your sister."

"No? I found the letters signed Kepley! Are you telling me she made them up herself?"

Thomas stared at Dalwood, a bleak look in his eyes. "I did not ruin your sister," he repeated.

Dalwood gave a grim laugh. "Oh, no. You promised her you would be together and then you took advantage of her and got her with child. But you claim you did not ruin her. Well, I suppose it may be so. I am perhaps the only person who knows why my sister took her own life.

But that, I tell you, is very small consolation and certainly not sufficient to outweigh my grief over her death. So beware, Kepley! I shall not forgive or forget what you did to her. And if I can pay you back in kind, I shall."

And then he left. Thomas stared after Dalwood, his face as impassive as he could contrive to keep it. Only when he heard the front door close behind his guest did he slowly make his way upstairs to Elizabeth. How far, he could not help but wonder, had Dalwood already gone toward his goal of revenge? And had Elizabeth been a willing partner?

Upstairs he found her in the room next to the nursery, pacing, not resting, clutching the locket at her throat. Abruptly, much of his anger fell away. He could see clearly the concern on her face for her son and without knowing that he did so, Thomas moved forward to comfort her, all thoughts of Dalwood set aside.

When she turned toward him, Thomas took her hands and said, "This need not fall on your shoulders alone. Not anymore. Dr. Brooks is staying for a few days. You may depend upon him to help your son."

It was too much to bear! Lisbeth pulled her hands free and rounded on Thomas, venting on him all her fury and frustration at being unable to do more to help her son.

"Dr. Brooks will *not* know what to do!" She all but spat the words. "None of them do. They come and stare and shake their heads and tell me to resign myself to putting his fate in God's hands! They tell me to resign myself to losing my son. But I will not! Do you hear me? I will not give him up, not without fighting for him with every breath I draw—and no physician will ever persuade me otherwise! I shall depend instead upon Aunt Margaret and her wisdom with herbs. At least she is able to ease the worst of his distress, and that is more than any physician has ever been able to do!"

"I did not know the matter was so serious," Thomas said gravely.

"It is!" she exclaimed, trying hard to keep her voice steady and failing. "They tell me not to hold too tight to my son, to accept that soon I may lose him. But I will not let him go! Not without a fight, at any rate. You, as a soldier, ought to understand."

He stared at her with a kindness that was her undoing. First one tear, and then another one, trickled down Lisbeth's cheek.

"I know that sometimes a battle cannot be won and the only sensible choice is to retreat, to accept defeat," Thomas answered, his voice scarcely louder than a whisper.

"And is that what you do?" she flung at him. "Do you always tamely accept defeat?"

"No."

One word, but it was enough. Lisbeth did not ask for more than that much understanding from him. Before she could think matters through, before she could stop the impulse, she walked into the arms he was holding open for her. And she wept as she had not allowed herself to weep since the first time a doctor told her that her son might not survive. Until this moment, she had had to be strong. Now she felt safe to feel the grief and fear that had been locked inside for so long.

Into her hair, she felt Thomas's breath as he murmured reassurances. "We shall consult the best physicians in London. We shall consult with every possible expert. We shall do everything we can to save your son."

Abruptly, Lisbeth felt as though a bucket of cold water had been dumped over her head. She pushed away from him. "My son," she echoed. "We shall do everything we can to save *my* son. Tell me," she said, her voice almost taunting him, "why are you so determined to believe he could not be your son as well? Tell me, what it is you think you see in his eyes or figure or hair or teeth that makes it so impossible for you to believe the truth?"

He looked taken aback. He started to stammer. Finally,

Kepley stopped and took a deep breath. Instead of answering her, he asked some questions of his own.

"How long have you known Dalwood? Does he often make himself free of the house?"

Lisbeth knew that Thomas was changing the subject. She knew she ought not to let him do so. But neither could she resist defending herself and her honor. The rumors, the whispered slander had cut too deep for far too long. In any event, she had a few questions of her own.

"Do you think I sought out his company?" Lisbeth demanded. She could not hide her anger, nor did she even try. "He came to this neighborhood not long after I did and sought me out! I kept him at arm's length; indeed, I still do. It is he who will not stop coming around to visit me."

"And you did not think to wonder just why he should be so kind?"

She had; of course she had. But Lisbeth was not about to say such a thing to Thomas. Not when he was questioning her honor.

Lisbeth shrugged and half turned away. "I was alone here, save for Aunt Margaret and a couple of servants too loyal to leave your service even though I could not pay them. Lord Peter was the only member of the *ton*, hereabouts, who did not give me the cut direct. More than that, he rode for a doctor once when Tom was ill and I had no one else to send. I did not care what his motives might be—I was too desperate for whatever help he could give."

"How desperate?"

Two words, but there was no mistaking his meaning. Lisbeth went very pale, but she did not turn and run. Instead, she looked him squarely in the eyes.

"However little you may wish to believe it, Tom is your son. I have never betrayed you—not with Lord Peter, nor with anyone else, not for any reason at any time." Elizabeth paused and her voice faltered, but then she tilted up her chin and went on defiantly. "You ask me about Dalwood, but what about his sister? Did you think I would not hear the rumors, Thomas? That no one would tell me about the two of you? Was she the woman your family wished you to marry? Did you father a child on her?"

He went pale, then, and as toplofty as his father. In the coldest of voices he said, "Yes, my parents wished me to marry Lady Anna Dalwood. But I was not the man who got her with child."

"But she was with child?"

Something crossed Thomas's face. Lisbeth would have sworn it was a flash of pain but not guilt. Instinctively she moved to put a hand on his arm. He looked at her, took a deep breath, and unbent a little.

"Think back," he said. "You knew me then. Did you ever see me dance attendance upon Lady Anna? Ever see me cast loverlike looks in her direction?"

"No," Lisbeth admitted. "Indeed, I should have said you avoided her company as much as you could."

He nodded. "I did. I knew my family hoped for a match, and neither she nor I wished to give them any cause to believe it might happen. Until the day my father told me she had agreed to the marriage. I did not know then that she was with child and afraid and needing to be married quickly."

"But who was the father? And why did he not marry her?" Lisbeth asked, bewildered.

Kepley looked over her head. He seemed to choose his words with great care. "I think we may assume," he told her, "that the father of her child could not marry her. And so the honor was to fall to me."

The bitterness in his voice was unmistakable and Lisbeth squeezed his arm in comfort. "I'm sorry," she said again. He looked at her and she went on. "Once we were friends, Thomas. I should like for us to be friends again—

just as you said you wanted as well. But if that is to happen, we must both let go of our poisonous suspicions."

He stared at her for a very long moment before he sighed. "I cannot," he said. "Not when I know that Tom cannot be my child."

She stared back at him and suddenly she could not bear to be in the room with him, could not bear to see the sadness in his eyes, the certainty that she had betrayed him. She let go of his arm and left the room as swiftly as she could without running.

Lisbeth would have gone into the nursery, but she knew from experience that Tom would sense her agitation and it would distress him, perhaps sufficiently to cause another attack. Instead, she headed down the stairs and outside toward the gardens.

Half an hour of pulling weeds, she told herself, would calm her rage. Half an hour of removing spent flowers would bring her back to the calm she knew she would need if she was ever to persuade her husband to listen to the truth.

But why should she try to persuade him? a tiny voice whispered to Lisbeth. Why not let Thomas think what he wished? If he did so, perhaps he would leave her alone. Then she could devote all her time to her son.

Perhaps Lisbeth would have listened to that voice, if she did not recall so well the friendship she and Thomas had once shared. And how much it had meant to her. If it were not still so clear in her mind how thoroughly he had entered into her sentiments when they were both in London and feeling set apart from the rest of the *ton*.

He had understood her then and confided in her things she was certain he had never told anyone else. And if that were not enough, Lisbeth could not help remembering her wedding night as well. She could not help wishing to know again the feel of his arms around her, and the closeness and pleasure they had shared. Indeed, there was a part of her that dearly wished to have it repeated. Not, however, when Thomas was in such a mood as he was today!

No, what Lisbeth wanted, what she craved, was the kindness, the sense of connection that had passed between them, and the joy they had found in each other's arms. And that could not happen if he was angry and disbelieved everything she said. It could not happen so long as Thomas denied his own son.

Miss Winsham stared down at Tom. His breathing seemed, for the moment at least, calmer. What, she wondered for what seemed the hundredth time, had Kepley seen or not seen when he looked at the child. Abruptly she came to a decision. Much as she disliked the man, Dr. Brooks was a physician. He might very well know things about the Kepley family that she and Elizabeth did not. It was, at any rate, worth asking.

Her decision made, Margaret gave instructions to the nursery maid and went in search of Dr. Brooks. He was not, as she supposed, in the library, but a footman sent her in the direction of the gardens.

Chapter 6

Thomas watched from the upstairs window as his wife, Elizabeth, knelt in the garden pulling weeds. So much for his campaign to seduce her! She was angrier with him than ever. Some distance beyond her, he could see Miss Winsham talking with Dr. Brooks. Thomas's gaze returned to his wife. Why couldn't she tell him the truth? If she did, it would make everything simple.

But things were not simple. When he looked at Tom he saw a dozen different possible fathers in the child's features—including himself. But that wasn't enough. Not when he knew the child lacked the birthmark every male child in the family was born with, for as long as anyone could remember. Granted, it faded by the second year, but it was always there at birth. Tom was not even a year old yet and he did not possess this birthmark.

No, the boy could not be his son and when he looked at him, Thomas could only think of Dalwood. He would indeed have had reason to wish to have revenge for his sister's sake. And yet, there would scarcely have been time, he thought, for Dalwood to father Tom. Not if he didn't know about the connection to a Kepley until after his sister died.

But perhaps he had suspected before then? Perhaps Dalwood had set out to get revenge through Elizabeth the moment Thomas left England? Once again Thomas cursed his father and his brother for placing him in such a situation!

But suppose it was not Dalwood who had fathered the boy. Then who? And just how quickly had Elizabeth sought solace elsewhere? To be sure, his ship had sunk soon after he left her. And perhaps in her grief she had simply sought comfort from some friend she knew. And perhaps that comfort had become something much more than she'd intended. Would he ever know the truth?

He looked out the window again. There was someone speaking to Elizabeth. Ah, it must be the new gardener. The fellow seemed to be telling her it was no longer her responsibility to tend the flowerbeds. It should never have been her responsibility, Thomas thought, and felt again the twinge of guilt at the circumstances in which he had found his wife. It was not how he had meant for things to be, not even if she had been unfaithful to him. And it was certainly not how he had arranged matters.

But he could not change the past; they could only go forward from here, and he had not done a very good job thus far. Thomas sighed. He had not meant to upset Elizabeth. He truly wanted to forgive her and begin anew, but she made it impossible! He was only human and he could not abide this deceit of hers. Perhaps if he had not counted so much on his faith in her, this betrayal would not hurt so much. But he had, and it did.

Thomas closed his eyes. Honor would not let him abandon Elizabeth again, no matter what she had done. Somehow, he would have to find a way past his own anger and patch matters up with her. Somehow he would have to find a way for them to become friends again. It was what they both wanted. And perhaps from friendship it would not be such an impossible step to man and wife.

He could insist, of course, upon his rights as her husband. Many a man would. But Thomas wanted more than physical ease. He wanted that sense of connection he had felt with Elizabeth upon their wedding night. He wanted to hear her laugh again, as she had laughed then. He wanted to see her smile as she had smiled just for him. He wanted to see her eyes turn dark with passion and hear the cry slip from her throat again, no matter how hard she tried to deny it.

She had not denied her cries that night. Nor the passion she had felt that matched his own. Thomas had not looked for such a gift when he'd asked her to marry him, but having experienced it once, he found himself reluctant to accept anything less than that from her now.

No. Somehow he must find a way to win back her affections. But he must do so without compromising his honor. He could promise to love the child and raise him as if the boy were his own, but he could not promise to believe the lie and he wished she would cease to ask it of him.

Abruptly, Thomas decided to go and talk with his batman. Odds were, George would be in the dressing room now, laying out Kepley's clothes for the evening.

He was. "Sir?" George said with some surprise when he saw Thomas.

"I wondered how you were getting on, below stairs, I mean, with the other servants," Thomas said lightly.

George hesitated. He chose his words with care. "I am a stranger here, sir. I am sure it is no wonder that they should be a trifle wary of me. Particularly as I am not the usual sort of gentleman's gentleman."

"Trouble?"

"None I can't handle, sir."

That gave Thomas pause. But he knew George well enough to suspect the other man spoke only the truth. He would find a way to handle any situation in which he found himself. He had certainly done so in the war.

"Do they ever speak of Lady Thomas?" he asked at last.

George regarded his employer with a shrewd look in his eyes. "Somewhat," he acknowledged. "Not to me directly, you understand, but to one another. Like her, they do. Aye, and respect her as well. And feel sorry for her circumstances while you was gone."

"I see."

Thomas hesitated, wondering how to ask his next question. George seemed to anticipate what it must be. "They would be betting below stairs, sir, on the father of young Tom, except they, one and all, agree it must be you, sir. They all believe her ladyship would never have done you a wrong turn, even if she did think you was dead."

"Do they?"

George met Thomas's gaze squarely. "Aye, sir, they do. Her ladyship has had callers, o'course. Gentlemen who thought p'rhaps her ladyship might be wanting company, if you see what I mean. They say she sent 'em all away with a flea in their ear. Including Dalwood. First time he's been here since then was today, and word is it was because he heard you was here and figured you wouldn't like the notion."

Thomas didn't quite know what to say to that. Fortunately, he didn't have to say anything. A footman appeared in the doorway of the dressing room.

"Sir?"

Thomas turned. "Yes?"

"Miss Winsham is asking that you speak with her, sir."

"In the nursery?"

"No, sir. She is waiting for you in the library."

"Very well. Tell her I shall be down directly."

"Yes, sir."

George carefully became engrossed once again in laying out Thomas's dinner clothes. Thomas left him alone. In the bedroom, he took a moment to look out one more time toward the gardens. Elizabeth was still speaking with the gardener and now they seemed to be smiling at each other.

Thomas grimaced. Somehow he did not think he and Miss Winsham would be smiling at each other. He remembered her only too well from the days when she chaperoned Elizabeth before their marriage. And what he remembered was a woman who brooked no nonsense from anyone. She had been fiercely protective of her niece then, and today he had seen her face down a respected physician. But he had never seen her gentle or amiable. What, he wondered, did she want with him now?

Thomas wondered if she meant to complain about the physician again or whether her cause was something else—such as his own treatment of her niece. Had Elizabeth told her? Perhaps. In any event, the older woman struck him as someone who was likely to know far more about his affairs than he wished!

He found Miss Winsham in the library, sitting in his favorite chair, perusing the pages of a text in Latin. She looked up at his entrance and he was reminded of nothing so much as one of his sister's governesses, the one they had called Dragon.

"You wished to speak with me?" Thomas asked with a calm he did not entirely feel.

"Yes. It is about my niece and your son. And the way you have handled matters thus far."

Thomas felt his expression harden. "That is between Elizabeth and myself," he replied. "I cannot think it proper to discuss the matter with you or anyone else."

"I see. That means you know you made a fool of yourself," Miss Winsham said dryly.

"I beg your pardon?"

"Don't come high in the instep with me!" she retorted roundly, as she rose to her feet. "I am, after all, only trying to help the pair of you. So far as I can see, you both possess a stubborn foolishness that ought to have been shaken out of you years ago and wasn't."

"If you are so concerned, then I suggest you speak to Elizabeth instead of to me," he said stiffly, refusing to retreat as she advanced toward him.

"I have already done so," Miss Winsham countered, "and now it is your turn."

"You do not comprehend the circumstances. . . ." Thomas began.

"I comprehend them very well," Miss Winsham contradicted him. "It is the lack of a mark, a birthmark to be precise, that distresses you."

Despite his intention to stand aloof, Thomas could not prevent her from seeing his start of surprise. "How do you know about the birthmark?" he asked.

She shrugged and smiled. It was not a very pleasant smile. "I ought to let you think I am a witch, the way so many other people do. But it is nothing of the sort. I listen and question and keep my wits about me. Apparently the birthmark is well enough known that Dr. Brooks has heard of it, though unfortunately not the physician who attended Elizabeth during her confinement."

"You had no right, Miss Winsham, to speak to an outsider about such matters!" Thomas said indignantly.

She glared at him. "And you, Lord Thomas, ought to be grateful that I did so, for otherwise your situation would be hopeless."

"I do not think it is hopeless," he answered defiantly. "As I have told Elizabeth, I am perfectly prepared to forgive her. I have thought over the matter and I can understand the circumstances of the child's conception."

"I should think you might," Miss Winsham retorted, "given that you were there!"

"If you know about the birthmark, then you know I was not," he ground out from between clenched teeth.

Miss Winsham gave him a withering glance and took an infuriating length of time before she answered. When she did, she spoke her words bluntly. "I know that you are the only possible father. If you do not believe my niece, if you cannot believe in her, then you have a problem. As for the birthmark, Elizabeth has the right to know that the lack of one is the source of your doubt."

"Are you going to tell her?"

"That, I should think, is up to you," Miss Winsham replied sternly. "You are a fool if you don't."

Something in his face changed and softened then. "Am I?" he asked. "Perhaps. But there is a part of me that wishes she would simply tell me the truth. Not because I have proof that Tom cannot be my child, but because she trusts me."

"You base everything on a birthmark," Miss Winsham said with a sigh. "But I have known birthmarks to skip a generation or two."

"Well, I have not," Thomas snapped back. "And it has never happened in my family!"

"No?" she said softly. "I wonder. In any event, you are foolish to so easily dismiss Elizabeth's regard for you. When we thought you were dead, there were men who offered for her hand. Men who swore they would take care of her—and her child. She refused them all. She lived here, scarcely managing to pay the worst of the creditors, when she could have been living in comfort elsewhere, married to any one of those men—including, perhaps, Dalwood."

Thomas turned away and looked out the windows that overlooked the front lawn. He ought to have come back sooner. He ought to have guessed how difficult it would be for Elizabeth. And yet, he had been raised to place honor above all else. How could he have abandoned duty simply to be with his wife?

Over his shoulder, Thomas asked, "Why didn't she marry any of them?"

Miss Winsham was silent so long he had to turn and look at her face. What he saw there almost undid him. "Do you think," she asked quietly, "that having given her heart to you, my niece could so easily have agreed to marry anyone else?"

"She did not marry me out of love, and well you know it!" Thomas countered angrily. "It was a marriage of convenience; nothing more."

"No? It began that way, I will allow. And I will even grant you that there was very little time for it to become anything more," Miss Winsham said with surprising gentleness in her voice. "But somehow, in that very short time, it did. Do you really think I have not seen how my niece looks at you? Or how you have looked at her? You may lie to yourselves, but do not, I pray, lie to me."

He flushed and looked away. Miss Winsham rose to her feet. When he did not speak she waited. Finally she shook her head. "You are, both of you, foolishly stubborn! One or both of you, Kepley, had better show some common sense, and soon, or you will forfeit all the kindness between you that you might otherwise have had. You might ask yourself if your pride—or whatever it is that keeps you from telling Elizabeth about the birthmark—is worth that!"

And then she marched out of the room, her displeasure left in the air behind her. Thomas sighed. He understood the sense of what she said, he just could not bring himself to actually believe it or to act upon her sage advice. Instead, he sat at the desk and tried without luck to focus his attention on the book Miss Winsham had left behind. That was where the physician found him, a short time later.

"My dear sir, you cannot mean to let that woman rule your household!"

Thomas looked at Dr. Brooks. "Which woman?" he asked, though he thought perhaps he knew.

"Miss Winsham!"

"What has she done now?"

"What has she not done?" the physician retorted. "I asked your cook to make up a medicinal concoction for the child, and Miss Winsham had the audacity to refuse to allow the child's nurse to give it to him!"

"Did Miss Winsham give a reason for such an impertinence?" Thomas asked.

"I am glad to see that you do recognize it as impertinence!" Dr. Brooks said, highly incensed. "She claimed that she could not allow it, if she was to prove that her methods were more efficacious than mine. She said that I must observe firsthand how well hers helped him, for only then, she claimed, would I be able to compare the results of my own interventions. The woman is mad, completely mad!"

"It would seem," Thomas said carefully, "that perhaps Miss Winsham has a point."

"It would seem," the physician ground out, "that Miss Winsham would rather attempt to prove herself right than know the child is getting the best possible care."

"But she disputes that your care would be better than hers."

Dr. Brooks waved a hand. "Obfuscation! She cannot possibly believe such a nonsensical notion! I am a doctor, trained at the university and under some of the best physicians in England. She is a woman; nothing more."

Thomas could not help but smile at the thought of Miss Winsham's reaction if she could have but heard Dr. Brooks's dismissal of her skills. "The lady would appear to believe the notion sufficiently to believe she has a chance of proving herself better than you," he pointed out gently. "I think she ought to have the chance."

"But it is your son!" Dr. Brooks protested. "It is your decision to make!"

Thomas hesitated. In theory Dr. Brooks was correct. Even if the child were fathered by someone else, so long as he chose to acknowledge it as his own, the right to determine the child's fate was also his. As angry as he was at Elizabeth, however, he could not do this to her.

In the end, he looked Dr. Brooks directly in the eye and said, "My wife and her aunt have had care of the boy all this time. I will not contradict their judgment at such a time as this."

Dr. Brooks stared at him for a long moment in disbelief. Then he snorted his disgust and turned to leave the room. As he went, Thomas could hear him muttering, "Mad! They are all fools or mad!"

Thomas very much hoped the fellow was wrong.

Chapter 7

If matters had been awkward before, they became even more so at dinner. In deference to Lord Thomas's return, both Miss Winsham and Lisbeth dressed for dinner. So, too, did Thomas.

Dr. Brooks, however, came to the dinner table dressed as he had been all day, for, as he explained it bluntly, "My housekeeper packed a bag for me, but she neglected to put in any finery, not thinking, you see, that if I was so desperately needed here that I must stay a few days, I would be needing such nonsense."

"It does not matter," Thomas assured him.

"No, of course it does not," Lisbeth agreed. "We are simply grateful to have you here at all."

Miss Winsham merely sniffed. "No one, save you, sir, even thought to worry," she said tartly. "None of us, I assure you, care one whit how you look!"

Just as tartly, Dr. Brooks replied, "Oh, now that reassures me immensely!"

How far matters might have gone, Lisbeth was relieved she need not find out, for the new butler came to announce that dinner was served. Never before had she been so pleased to hear those words!

Thomas escorted her in to dinner and it was a strange feeling, to be holding his arm again. Her hand trembled slightly, but he did not seem to notice and for that Lisbeth was grateful.

As they sat, some of the tension seemed to go out of

Dr. Brooks. He turned his attention to Thomas. "How long were you away, sir?"

"Twenty months."

The words were spoken with gritted teeth, but Dr. Brooks seemed not to notice. He merely nodded and said, "For how much of that time were you a prisoner of war?"

As Thomas had just started to take a sip of wine, this resulted in his having to be thumped on the back by Lisbeth, who was closest to hand.

"You were a prisoner of war?" she asked, when he regained his composure again.

Thomas colored up. He glared at Dr. Brooks. "Do you not think," he asked icily, "that it is for me to decide whether or not this is a topic I wish to pursue?"

Dr. Brooks waved a hand. "I have no social graces; never did. My concern is for my patients."

"I am not your patient."

Brooks smiled. "Can't help m'self. Everyone is a patient to me. And it is obvious to me that you ought to be talking about it, if you were a prisoner of war."

"Not at the dinner table. Not in front of ladies," Thomas managed to say with a forbidding look upon his face.

Under the table, Lisbeth found herself patting his knee in reassurance. Thomas started in surprise, then looked at her with confusion and perhaps a trace of gratitude as well. And a little of his anger seemed to abate. But it was Aunt Margaret who truly took charge.

"My dear doctor," she said, staring at him as though he were someone who ought to be humored, "no one could mistake your manners for those of a gentleman, but perhaps you could at least pretend?"

Lisbeth thought that Dr. Brooks was going to suffer an attack of apoplexy. His face turned an alarming shade of red. He sputtered as he answered her aunt, and his voice was shaking with unmistakable anger.

"I will have you know, madam, that my pedigree is undoubtedly at least as good as yours. I am a Brooks of Brooks Hall, even if I did choose to study medicine!"

Aunt Margaret merely snorted. "And I am a Winsham, and my niece is late of Henley Hall."

It was Dr. Brooks's turn to snort. "I should not like to boast of a connection to the late Lord Henley. Hide it, perhaps, but not boast."

In a voice held tightly in check, Lisbeth managed to ask, "Did you know my father, sir?"

The sight of her pale face seemed to recall Dr. Brooks to himself and to his situation. He colored up again, but his response was as blunt as ever. "Years ago, as a young doctor, I was summoned to Henley Hall with Dr. Parr, with whom I had just begun to work."

"I do not remember such a visit," Aunt Margaret objected.

He glared at her. "Nevertheless, Miss Winsham, I was there!" Brooks looked again at Lisbeth and went on in a kindly voice, "We were asked to treat Lady Henley, and all I can say is that I left the place wishing I could plant his lordship a facer for the way he behaved toward her. I heard she died not so very long after that. I remember because Lord Henley used her death as an excuse not to pay the fee he had promised." Almost as an afterthought he added, "I hope I have not offended you. You are nothing like your father, I assure you."

Lisbeth almost smiled at that. "No, I think I am not. And I can well imagine my father behaving in just such a horrible way. But if you are of such a good family, how did you come to be a physician? Did your family not object?"

"Of course they objected!" Dr. Brooks replied, a twinkle now in his eyes. "But I could scarcely let that stop me from doing what I wished."

"Clearly a man of resolution," Lisbeth murmured.

"Clearly a fool!" Aunt Margaret retorted, her voice a trifle louder than her niece's.

But Dr. Brooks was more amused than otherwise. "Perhaps," he told her amiably. "But far less a fool than a lady who allows herself to become eccentric."

Aunt Margaret's eyes narrowed in a dangerous way and Lisbeth made haste to intercede. "You still have not told us how you came to be a physician."

He waved a hand carelessly. "Oh, as to that, I was always interested in science as a boy. Whenever our own physician would come to call upon any member of the household, I would pester him with questions. He thought, I am sure, that I would soon become bored. Instead I discovered it was, above all things, what I wished to do with my life."

The words fell into the respectful silence and for once even Aunt Margaret forbore to roast him. Instead, she cleared her throat and said, with some intensity of emotion, "Perhaps we are not so very different after all."

Dr. Brooks looked startled, but determined to keep the unexpected and sudden peace. He turned the talk to other matters and Lisbeth began to think things would be well after all. That was when a footman once more appeared to summon her urgently to her son.

Aunt Margaret was a scant two steps behind Lisbeth, and the men were right behind her. They mounted the stairs as swiftly as possible. In the nursery they found that the nursery maid had already put a pot of water over the fire to bring it to a boil and was setting up a tent very much like the one Lisbeth and Aunt Margaret had contrived earlier in the day. Even from the hallway they could hear Tom's labored breathing.

Margaret pulled out the herbs she always kept handy for this purpose and put a net bag of them into the pot. Lisbeth went to hold her son. As she murmured softly to him, he seemed to settle down a little, though his breathing still sounded harsh and came with a struggle. Dr. Brooks was at her side almost before she had her son in her lap and he was listening to the child's breathing, looking into his eyes, and speaking to the child himself.

The moment the water was boiling, Lisbeth and Tom and Dr. Brooks and the pot all went into the tent. Dr. Brooks continued to examine Tom, and Lisbeth was forced to keep her tongue between her teeth, for otherwise she would have screamed at him not to fret her child.

But Tom liked Dr. Brooks and, as the steam worked its magic, he even managed to smile at the man. When Lisbeth coaxed him to drink a mug of the tea and his breathing eased even more, he was able to look at Dr. Brooks with great curiosity. And for that, Lisbeth was very grateful. Anything that distracted her son from his discomfort was something—or someone—to be cherished.

When he was recovered sufficiently, Lisbeth and Dr. Brooks and Tom climbed back out of the tent and she sat on the bed next to her son. She found his favorite book, one of the ones written by her sister Tessa, and began to read about a shy dragon. He sat enthralled and before the story was done, his eyes had closed and he was asleep.

The nursery maid helped Lisbeth to tuck Tom into bed. "I'll watch over him, ma'am," the woman whispered, "and call you at once if you are needed."

Lisbeth nodded. She knew from experience that her son would sleep for hours. She led the group back downstairs. Dinner still waited on the table, but no one had an appetite anymore.

"Clear it away," Thomas told the servants.

"We shall see you in the drawing room after you have had your brandy," Lisbeth told Thomas and Dr. Brooks.

But Dr. Brooks had other notions. "I'll just come along with you," he said. "I wish to ask Miss Winsham more about the herbs she brewed in that pot. They seemed remarkably efficacious and I wish to know precisely how they are grown and where and what amount you use and . . ."

Lisbeth watched as Dr. Brooks and her aunt started off down the hall toward the drawing room. When she looked at Thomas, he smiled wryly at her. "There is no point to my staying here either. Nor would I wish to, anyway. How are you doing, Elizabeth? It cannot be easy to watch your son go through such trials."

For once she did not argue his choice of words. She was far too tired to do so. "It is not easy," she agreed. "Each time, I worry that perhaps this will be the time his breathing will not recover. Each time I worry that this will be the time I lose my son."

She started to cry then, and he put his arms around her, oblivious to the interested stares of the servants. In this moment, Lisbeth was the only person who mattered. And she needed him.

The tears flowed freely now, drenching his jacket. But he didn't care. He murmured soothing words to the top of her head and made all sorts of vows, including that he would find a way to save her son. But she balked at that one.

Lisbeth pulled back and looked up at Thomas. "I know that you mean well," she said. "And I shall never stop fighting for our son's life. But do not make promises you cannot keep. And you cannot keep that one."

He would have argued, but something in her eyes stopped him. Instead he said, quietly, seriously, "When I was a prisoner of war, they told me I might never see home again. They said that if I did, it would all seem different. They tried to tell me I was a fool to hang on to hope. But I am home now. As impossible as it sometimes seemed, I did survive. I do believe in miracles."

She searched his eyes for a very long time. At last she said, "Will you tell me, sometime, what it was like? Will you tell me what happened to you?"

He hesitated and then reluctantly agreed. "Sometime," he agreed. "But not just yet."

She wanted to argue; he could see it in her eyes. But

she didn't. Instead she smiled a tearful smile and said, "We'd better go join Dr. Brooks and Aunt Margaret before they come to blows."

Thomas chuckled. "I suspect you are right. Two worse-matched people I have never seen! But one thing first," he said.

He kissed her. Slowly, gently, and then, as she responded to his kiss, with growing need. Her arms slipped up around his neck and she did not protest when he arched her close to his body.

When he let her go, she stared up at him a moment in dazed confusion. "I will not wait forever," he warned her.

She swallowed hard and nodded, but she did not say she was ready and so Thomas turned away first. "Come," he said. "Let us see if the doctor and Miss Winsham have come to daggers drawn yet."

But they had not come to blows. They were not even fighting. Indeed, they were deep in conversation, avidly sharing experiences so that both Thomas and Lisbeth felt very much de trop. Still, the moment the younger couple entered the drawing room, the older pair immediately broke off their conversation.

"You seem to have reached some sort of accord," Kepley suggested carefully.

Dr. Brooks harrumphed. "Well, perhaps she is not such a foolish creature as I thought. And her methods are not quite so nonsensical as those of most of her kind."

"Most of my kind?" Aunt Margaret echoed with raised eyebrow.

"Er, you know, women," Dr. Brooks protested. "You know that most of your sex cannot think in any sort of scientific manner."

"I know that most of them have never been given the chance to try!" Aunt Margaret shot back.

"Has your niece been given the chance to try?"

"Her interests run to other directions."

"Of course they do. Precisely my point."

Aunt Margaret started to splutter with indignation and Lisbeth judged it time to intervene. "It is not kind of you, sir, to roast my aunt. Particularly since it is evident that you do respect her knowledge."

"In this case, at any rate," Dr. Brooks grudgingly conceded. "And she does seem to have found some interesting uses for certain herbs and such. Of course, someone ought to determine scientifically whether or not they are consistently useful. . . ."

"I have done so!" Aunt Margaret exclaimed indignantly. "I told you I should be happy to share with you my records on that score."

It was Thomas who managed to keep them from coming to blows by suggesting a game of cards. That was quite sufficient to chase them all from the room and upstairs to their beds.

Or most everyone went to bed, at any rate. Lisbeth allowed her maid to undress her and then, as she had done the night before, she crept to the small room where she did her work. There she lit several candles, picked up needle and thread, and worked steadily for several hours on the gown and the petticoats she had promised Mrs. Parker.

It wasn't really a hardship. Lisbeth loved the feel of the silks and satins and velvets. At the same time, she could not also help but feel a strong degree of envy for the women who would wear these gowns. Indeed, during these past months, whenever she worked on a gown she would try to imagine where it would be worn. Was it a young lady? Would some gentleman fall in love with her when she was wearing the dress that Lisbeth had made?

But she didn't need to feel envy any longer, she told herself. Now that Thomas was back, she would be able to order just such gowns herself. No longer would she have to sew whatever she wished to wear. He would want her to dress well. That meant she could order the silks and satins and velvets she loved. It was a very strange thought.

Lisbeth smiled wistfully. Once she would have been able to tell Thomas just such thoughts as these and known he would understand. But somehow it all seemed different, now that they were married. Somehow she still didn't dare tell him how she had made ends meet while he was gone.

Perhaps she was foolish. Perhaps it wouldn't matter if Thomas found out. Perhaps he would understand. But perhaps he would not. The independent streak in her that he had found charmingly eccentric in a young lady he called a friend, he might very well consider outrageous in his wife. And if there was one thing Lord Aylsham had impressed upon Lisbeth when he saw her, it was the consequence due the Kepley family name. Certainly the marquess would never forgive her, if he found out. And after his kindness today, Lisbeth could not, she found, risk that Thomas would feel the same.

She never knew that as she stitched the satin and velvet fabrics, Thomas stood outside her bedroom door, candle in hand. Or that half a dozen times he started to knock on that door, to see if perhaps, despite everything between them, she would welcome him to her bed tonight.

She never knew that in the end he slipped silently back to his own room and his now lonely bed and lay awake thinking of her—remembering their wedding night.

Chapter 8

Tom was much improved in the morning. So much so that Dr. Brooks once again expressed his approval to Aunt Margaret. An urgent message called him to another patient and he took his leave, not expecting to return. "For," as he told her with a smile, "you have quite convinced me of your skills, and I do need to return home."

When he left the house, it was with a recipe in his hands for the herbal brew Miss Winsham had concocted. If she seemed to regret the doctor's departure, she did not say so, but there was a wistful look in her eyes for the rest of the day.

Meanwhile, Lisbeth found Thomas in the study. He held a letter that seemed to be troubling him a great deal. At the sight of her, he tried to smile.

"Does Tom often suffer from such attacks?" he asked abruptly.

"Sometimes. It is very hard to predict. So much depends upon the weather and whether he has recently caught cold," Lisbeth replied.

"Is he well enough to travel?"

"Yes, I think so, but why?"

"We must go to London as soon as possible," Thomas said, "and I wish to take him with us."

"Why?"

He rose to his feet and clasped his hands behind him. "I told you before that I wish the *ton* to see us as a fam-

ily—a happy, loving family. The sooner we go to London
and let them see us together, the better."

"Why, Thomas?"

He stared at her as though he thought that would be
enough to silence her question. It wasn't. Lisbeth stared
back with just as great a determination. In the end, it was
Kepley who yielded. He sighed, and then he told her.

"I have had a letter from a friend. From your sister's
husband, in fact, Lord Rivendale. He tells me the gossip
has gotten worse since I returned from the continent and
he urges me to come to London as soon as possible with
you and the child to prove it false."

"When?"

"Tomorrow—if we can be ready by then."

Lisbeth drew in a deep breath. Mrs. Parker would not
be happy. Nor would it be easy to pack up the household
in such a short time. And she was not certain she was
ready to face London and the *ton* just yet.

But in the end, she only said, "We can try."

Thomas nodded. Lisbeth started to leave the room and
he stopped her. "Are you truly content with this? Your
son really is well enough to travel?" he asked. "And you
really do not mind?"

She hesitated, but honesty was too strong a habit for
her to lie to him. "I shall be glad to see my sisters again.
And their children."

He came over to Lisbeth, then, and touched the side of
her cheek. Without meaning to, she leaned into his touch.
She wished she had the courage to reach out to touch
him. But he was talking again.

"And have you no desire to go to balls or parties?" he
asked. His voice held curiosity and something else. "Do
you never think of the theater? Do you not dream, perhaps, of dancing? Would you not wish to dance with me?"

His hand was still stroking her cheek and that made it
so hard to think! And when he spoke of dancing she could
imagine very well his hand holding hers, leading her

through the figures of the dance. Perhaps even twirling about the floor in a waltz. The thought brought a blush to her cheeks and she thought she would like it very much. But she hesitated, concern for him uppermost in her mind.

"I, that is, the last time we were in London together you could not dance, because of the injury to your leg," Lisbeth said, looking up into Thomas's eyes. "Is it sufficiently healed for you to dance now?"

He nodded and Lisbeth found herself smiling wistfully. "Then I think I would like to dance with you."

"Good, for I should like to dance with you." Abruptly his hand fell away from her face and he turned back to his desk. His voice became brisk as he said, "Very well. We leave tomorrow, or as soon as may be."

Upstairs, Lisbeth found Aunt Margaret looking into her cupboard. "We shall both need to visit a mantua maker when we get to London," she told her niece briskly. "It is time and past that we improved our wardrobes."

Lisbeth started. "How did you know?"

"Know what?"

"That we were going to London?"

Aunt Margaret ticked off the reasons on the tips of her fingers. "Kepley has returned and now we have the funds to go to London. It is the Season. There have been rumors he must have heard and will wish to contradict. I presume Tom goes with us?"

In spite of herself, in spite of how long and how well she had known her aunt, Lisbeth was startled at her perspicacity. "Quite correct," she agreed. "We are going to London and Tom does go with us."

Aunt Margaret nodded approvingly. "Excellent. That will put paid to the rumors faster than anything else could have done. I am glad your husband is showing such good sense. How soon does he wish for us to leave for the city?"

"Tomorrow."

"That is not a great deal of time," Miss Winsham said.

She hesitated. "What about the work you were to do for Mrs. Parker?"

Lisbeth took a deep breath. "I have finished most of it. Mrs. Parker will simply have to find someone else to do the rest. Now that it is no longer essential to earn funds to pay for the food on our table, I must admit I shall be glad to be quit of the sewing."

"Does *he* know?"

Lisbeth shook her head. "No, and if we are fortunate he need never know what shifts to which we were forced while he was gone. At least I do not wish to have to tell him until matters are better between us."

Miss Winsham hesitated. "You know that in general I strongly believe that secrets are not wise between a man and wife," she said. "And yet, I must confess that in your place I should probably also keep my counsel." She paused, then asked, "Has Kepley spoken at all about why he does not believe Tom to be his son?"

Lisbeth shook her head. "No. He only talked about how we needed to go to London to confound the gossip there."

It seemed to Lisbeth that her aunt sighed. But then Miss Winsham took a brisker tone. "I must confess that I shall be glad to be in London again. It is not that I begrudge being here," she added hastily. "You and Tom needed me and I have been back there several times."

"But you miss working with the children your friends rescued," Lisbeth said shrewdly. "You miss taking part in the rescue work yourself."

"Yes," Aunt Margaret agreed. "Oh, I know that we have done some good here. But it is not the same. I have felt very isolated these past months."

"You were isolated when you lived in your cottage near Henley Hall," Lisbeth pointed out.

Miss Winsham shook her head. "I had lived there long enough that I had some few friends. And I was needed, not just to help rescue children, but for my healing. Here, save for you, no one wishes to trust my skills. No, it is not the same. I shall be glad to see London again. And after that, well, it will be time, I suppose, for me to return to my cottage in the woods."

"Aunt Margaret!" Lisbeth exclaimed, not trying to hide her dismay. "But I need you!"

"For the moment you do," Miss Winsham agreed gently, "because you and Kepley still need to become reacquainted with each other. And because Tom is so ill. But we may hope the boy will grow out of some of the trouble, or I shall teach your nursery staff what to do. You and Kepley will come to an understanding, and then, perhaps, it will be time for me to go. But you need not look so worried, Elizabeth, it will not happen for a little while yet."

"What if we can't resolve matters, Thomas and I?" Lisbeth whispered, clutching the locket at her throat.

Miss Winsham smiled. "You will. Because you must. Sooner or later, you will each find the courage to tell the other the truth."

Lisbeth wanted to ask her aunt what she meant, but there was something about the older woman's manner that stopped her. And then the moment was lost. Miss Winsham had turned away.

Briskly she said, "At any rate, we had best get ready to go to London. You will want to inform the servants, Elizabeth, for they will need to know as soon as possible. Don't forget to tell the new nursery maid to pack up all of little Tom's things, including his favorite toys. And I shall write a letter to Dr. Brooks to let him know that we are leaving."

"Write to Dr. Brooks?" Lisbeth echoed, taken aback. "Why on earth should you write to him?"

"Because," Aunt Margaret began, carefully avoiding her niece's shrewd eyes, "I promised to let Dr. Brooks know how Tom goes on. And he ought to be informed we are removing to London so that he is not dismayed if there is some delay in hearing from me."

"I see."

"You see nothing of the sort!" Miss Winsham retorted with some asperity. "Now go and pack!"

Lisbeth went, smiling to herself. It was odd to see Aunt Margaret flustered, and stranger still to know that it was because of a man. And yet it was a comforting notion that even her aunt was subject to such emotions. For the past twenty months, indeed, for most of her life, Lisbeth had been accustomed to think the older woman invincible.

By the time she went downstairs, after speaking to the nursery maid, she found that word had already spread, in the mysterious way that it does among servants, and preparations were already in hand for the journey. There was very little for her to do.

Lisbeth found herself wandering out to the gardens, where she had spent so much time. Now there were no more weeds to be pulled; the new staff was far too efficient for that. And the spent flowers had been removed to encourage new ones to blossom. Even bushes had been pruned that were long overdue for such treatment.

She ought to have been pleased, Lisbeth told herself. And she was, of course, but she also felt a bit at loose ends. For so long she had had to struggle so hard to manage everything herself that now that she had a staff of servants to do things for her, she did not quite know how to cope with the change in her circumstances.

But perhaps the biggest part of the trouble was that Lisbeth was at a loss as to how to accustom herself to her husband's presence in her household. Particularly since he had the power to simply say to her: "We are going to London. Tell the servants to pack."

And it would only get worse. Thomas was a man, and as an officer he was also accustomed to giving commands. How soon before he tried to dictate to her how she ought to behave? How soon before he tried to tell her what she must think and feel and do? Thus far, Thomas had been more kind than not, but would that last? When would he start to become impatient with her, as her father had been with her mother? When would he start to object to the things she wished to do?

It was a question to which Lisbeth found she did not wish to know the answer. She could only hope that her fears were mistaken and Thomas would prove himself to be the man she thought he was when they married. Unfortunately, short of waiting to see, there was no way for her to know.

She was still staring at the roses when Thomas found her. "Elizabeth?"

She started and turned to face him. "Is something wrong?"

He drew in a deep breath; then he smiled the whimsical, lopsided grin that had first drawn her to him. "It occurred to me," he said, "that I might have seemed a trifle high-handed, and I thought, perhaps, you had a right to know why."

He held something out to her and she realized it was the letter from Lord Rivendale. She took it gingerly, not entirely certain she wished to know what her sister's husband had written. But she read the letter anyway, her anger growing with each line. When she was done, she handed it back to Thomas, not troubling to hide her feelings.

"So the *ton* thinks your marriage was a mistake, easily undone? Some of your friends are prepared to swear whatever might be needed? They have connections that will help them to accomplish this generous deed? They have, in fact, already set in motion certain steps to see that all is made easy for you to do so?" Lisbeth quoted from the letter.

He smiled thinly. "Now you understand the urgency of our journey to London. And the need for the *ton* to see that we are truly wed and wish to stay so."

She searched his face for a very long moment. "Why?" she asked.

He frowned. "What do you mean?"

She chose her words with care. "Why do you wish to

do this? I know that you married me because otherwise your family would have forced you to marry someone else. But now you believe I have been unfaithful to you. Why, then, would you not be happy to do as your friends suggest and have our marriage undone? Why would you not be happy to be free of me, and of my child? Then you could marry whomever you wished."

Thomas took a long time to answer, so long that she began to fear her words had touched too close to home and that he would not answer. But when he did speak, the words were chosen with as great care as her own had been, and his voice held a gentleness she did not expect.

"Do you wish to be free of me?" he asked. She shook her head, and after a moment he went on. "No more do I wish to be free of you. I remember, you see, our wedding night. Yes, I know I am putting you to the blush. But that night is what kept my resolution firm when others around me gave up hope of ever seeing England again. That night was what kept my wits from deserting me when others were losing theirs. I have thought about you, Elizabeth, every day for twenty months. Do you wonder, then, that having returned and found you here, I am not willing to give you up?"

She leaned toward him without even realizing she did so, drawn by the kindness, the gentleness, the love she heard in his voice. But she hesitated as well. There was so much between them, so many secrets, and so much suspicion. He didn't believe that Tom was his son. She had not yet found the courage to tell him about Mrs. Parker. He had not told her about the time he was gone. And yet, a part of her desperately wanted to believe they could be happy together anyway.

But she waited too long to answer. "I see," he said, bitterness in his voice as he turned away.

"Thomas!"

He stopped but did not turn to face Lisbeth as she

called his name. Instead, he waited. She searched for the right words to say.

"Thomas, we have been apart twenty months. It will take time for us to get to know each other again. Time to learn to trust each other. But I dearly hope that we will. There is nothing that would please me more."

He nodded, as though he did not trust himself to speak, and after a moment he started for the house without looking to see if she followed.

With a tiny sigh, Lisbeth did so. Indeed, she would have followed him to his study and tried to talk with him more, but the new steward he had hired was there and he needed to talk with him instead.

Lisbeth made her way upstairs to the parlor she used for her sewing. She had better get everything ready for Mrs. Parker. She would hear the news very soon, if she had not heard it already, and she would want to come and collect the gowns Lisbeth was working on for her.

And in a way, part of her hoped that Thomas would come in search of her as well and find her finishing up the last of the stitching. Because if he found her here, at her needle, then Lisbeth would have to tell him about the sewing. And it would mean one less secret between them.

It occurred to Lisbeth that she could simply go and tell Thomas about it. He might very well understand. But what if he did not? The thought that she might push him even farther away was more than she could bear.

Thomas wanted to go in search of his wife. But duty demanded that he first make certain his tenants were provided for. There were orders to be given to the new steward—particularly if he and Elizabeth were going to be gone from the estate for some time.

But then he would have gone in search of her. Except that he found himself thinking of Miss Winsham's words from the day before. She thought he ought to tell Eliza-

beth about the birthmark. Was she right? Was it only
pride that kept him from doing so?

It was a lowering thought. He wanted to make matters
work between Elizabeth and himself. But he also needed
the safe haven he had dreamed of while he was away at
war. He wanted the Elizabeth he once had known, the
woman who believed in him, trusted him, and would
speak the truth to him, no matter what the cost to herself.

But Thomas wanted more than that. He also wanted
the Elizabeth who would welcome him at night, holding
him close and loving him, as passionately as she had on
their wedding night. Already he thought that perhaps it
might soon be possible. Each day she seemed to look at
him with a little more longing and a little less fear in her
eyes. She did not draw away when he reached out to
touch her. But he was afraid to press her too hard.

And so he did not go in search of her. Let her wonder
where he was and perhaps even begin to miss his company. Let her, perhaps, come in search of him.

She ought to be glad to be going back in London, Margaret told herself as she packed. It would be even better,
of course, if she were returning to her old cottage in the
woods. But she could not do that until she knew things
would work out between Kepley and Elizabeth and that
Tom would be all right.

She paused and took a deep breath. It was not, Margaret told herself stoutly, the thought of a certain gruff
physician that made her reluctant to leave. It couldn't be,
for that would be foolish beyond permission. But she
took extra care to make certain the letter she had written
him would be posted.

Chapter 9

London. It was a city that held all sorts of emotions for Lisbeth. Here, years ago, her father had hoped to sell her to the highest bidder and failed. Here she had met Thomas and he had married her and shown her what joy there might be found in such a state. Here she would have to face, once again, all the rumors, all the slights, and all the heartache of the days after he had left and she thought he was dead. She had not been back since before Tom was born.

As he sat beside her, Thomas could not help but think of the last time he had been there. Right around his trip to Portugal. And that seemed a lifetime away. He, too, found himself thinking of his wedding day and wondering what sort of reception they would find.

Was Elizabeth afraid? He would have liked to offer her comfort. But there was something in her manner that kept him at arm's length, almost as if he were a stranger. And because it hurt that she could treat him in such a way, even though he was her husband, Thomas turned his thoughts to the child she held on her lap.

Elizabeth chatted to her son about all the things he might see while they were in London. And Thomas found himself wishing she would smile at him the way she smiled at her son. But he also felt relief. So far, the child's health did not seem impaired by the journey. Tom was livelier than Thomas could recall seeing him since he came home. He only hoped the air in London would not prove detrimental to the boy.

As for Miss Winsham, she sat in her corner of the carriage, looking out the window, expressing her disapproval of the city in the way she sat and periodically sniffing in disdain as one disagreeable odor or another assailed their senses.

"When are they going to clean the streets?" she demanded at last.

"Never, I should think," Lisbeth retorted equably. "Or, at any rate, no better than they already do. You can see that almost every corner has a boy with homemade broom willing to sweep the street clean before the footsteps of a gentleman or his lady."

As someone chose that unfortunate moment to hurl some refuse into the street, Miss Winsham, quite correctly, was not impressed with her niece's reasoning. She merely sniffed again and lapsed back into silence.

Thomas wished he could reach over and squeeze his wife's hand. He wished that he and Elizabeth were on terms that such a gesture would seem natural. He wished that the child on her lap were his son so that he could have held the child and shown him the passing sights and helped to plan what treats might be in store for him.

As if she read his thoughts, Elizabeth looked at Kepley. There was a deep sadness in her eyes as she studied him, then looked down at her son, who sat happily sheltered on her lap. Tom was supposed to be in the other carriage. But he had kicked up such a fuss when the attempt was made to place him there, instead of with his mother, that the traveling party had unanimously agreed to allow him to ride with Elizabeth. Fortunately, he was a very good traveler. Tom was perfectly happy to stare out the window of the carriage at the passing scene. Now he crowed with laughter at the sights before his young eyes.

Soon enough, the carriage drew to a halt before an elegant town house. It was an old-fashioned structure, but that was its very charm, for it was far larger than any house being built in London now. Certainly, it had plenty of room, not just for the Marquess and Marchioness of Aylsham, but for each of their sons' and daughters' families to visit, as well.

Thomas had not told Elizabeth where they would be staying while in London, and she had not thought to ask. He saw the precise moment when she realized where they were headed. She turned her face to him with a shocked look and an unspoken question in her eyes. He looked away, grateful that the carriage was already pulling to a halt and there would be no time for any objections.

In moments, a footman opened the carriage door and set down the steps. He helped Miss Winsham descend first and then she reached for Tom, to take him so that Elizabeth could step down as well.

"Thomas," she asked in a dangerously soft voice, as they both moved toward the doorway of the carriage, "why are we stopping here?"

"This is where we will stay while we are in London."

"No!"

"Yes."

He did not hesitate, but gave her a tiny push so that Elizabeth was forced to step down to the street, and he followed immediately. Then, before she could protest further, Thomas was leading her up the steps of the town house, leaving Miss Winsham to follow as best she could with the child.

Softly, so that the servants and interested onlookers could not overhear, Elizabeth began to berate him. "I do not want to stay in your parents' house!" she said. "They cannot abide me, nor I them. Surely we are not so penurious that we cannot afford to hire an establishment for the few weeks we shall be here?"

He ignored the plea in her voice, the look of betrayal in her eyes. In truth, Thomas was no happier with the solution than she was. But it was, he told himself, the best possible thing to do. He tried to explain it to her.

"We are staying in my parents' home," he replied, just as softly, "because it is the one thing that will confound all the rumors flying about London. Trust me, Elizabeth, when I say that my parents will be no more pleased than you are to have us descend upon them unannounced like this. They will be no more pleased than you are to discover that they must at least pretend to complacency. If you can think of no other way to reconcile yourself to these circumstances, at least think of how much discomfort your presence here will bring to them! Can you think of any better revenge?"

Despite Elizabeth's anger, that surprised a spurt of laughter from her. Then she said, "Very well. But if we end by your father casting you off entirely, be forewarned that I shall remind you that I told you it would be so."

There was no more time to talk. The most toplofty butler in London was opening the front door. His air of disdain, however, was instantly replaced with one of welcome as he recognized Thomas.

"Sir!" he said with obvious pleasure in his voice. "The Marquess and Marchioness will be delighted to see you back here so soon!"

"Will they?" Thomas asked dryly. "I hope you may be right. This is my wife, Lady Thomas, and her aunt, Miss Winsham, and my son, Tom."

If this very elegant butler felt the slightest dismay at the unexpected invasion, he did not say so. Instead he bowed and greeted them, and promptly directed them into the rose-colored parlor.

"You may be comfortable and private here until your rooms can be prepared," he explained. "I shall have a tray with some tea and refreshments sent straight in."

He turned to go and Thomas stopped him. "My parents?" he asked quietly.

The butler drew in a deep breath. "Lord and Lady Aylsham are not here, though they do plan to dine alone at home tonight. I believe the marquess has gone to his club for the afternoon. The marchioness is making calls. You have, I venture to say, some three hours or more before they return."

A look passed between the two men and they almost smiled. But that would not have been proper and the moment was gone. Thomas turned to Elizabeth and her aunt.

"I daresay that long before my parents return we will be nicely settled into our rooms. And Tom will be able to have his nap."

"Marshaling your troops for the assault, sir?" Miss Winsham asked dryly.

Thomas grinned unrepentantly. "Would you expect anything less of me? Indeed, I begin to wonder if perhaps I ought not to invite some friends to join us. Or, no, perhaps that would be unwise. Better, if there is to be an uproar, that only family be present as witnesses."

Elizabeth glared at him. "Had you thought to inform your parents of our impending arrival, perhaps there might not be an uproar."

Thomas shook his head. His voice was grim as he replied, "Oh, yes, there would have been."

The tea arrived just then, saving him from further argument. Elizabeth turned her attention to feeding her son, but she still looked at Thomas, from time to time, with a troubled look in her eyes. He understood, but how could he tell her that he was as afraid of staying at his parents' London town house as she was and that only her presence at his side gave him the courage to do so?

Thomas watched as Elizabeth bent to the task of coaxing her son into eating. By the time she had done so, the housekeeper came to show them to their rooms. First they left Tom in the nursery and he seemed quite pleased to be there, for it was not so very different from his nursery at home. Particularly as his toys had already been unpacked and placed in the room where he would be sleeping.

Then the housekeeper showed Miss Winsham to her room. Finally she led Thomas and Elizabeth to the suite of rooms set aside for them. They were large and airy and elegantly furnished. His own things had been placed in the largest room and he knew his wife's would be in another. From the look the housekeeper gave them, it was evident she thought he would be pleased by such an arrangement.

Thomas stopped her from leaving. In a languid voice that caused Elizabeth to turn and look at him sharply, he said, "Please have someone move my wife's things into this room. We will share it."

"Her ladyship won't approve," the housekeeper warned him. "Your brothers and their wives don't share a room."

"Nonetheless, my wife and I shall do so," Thomas told her gently but firmly.

"But what am I to tell your parents?" the housekeeper asked with some distress.

"Whatever you wish. You need not, after all, inform them of how we are using the rooms set aside for us. Let them assume whatever they wish."

The housekeeper grimaced but allowed the wisdom of his suggestion. The moment she was gone, Elizabeth turned to Thomas.

"Why did you tell her we were going to share a room?" she asked slowly. "Even if you wished us to do so, why would you wish to make such a point of the matter?"

He was tired, so very tired, and not in the least in the mood to fight with her. So now he met Elizabeth's gaze and said, with blunt honesty, "The housekeeper will not tell my parents we are sharing a room, but she will tell the other servants. And they will tell their friends and their friends will tell their masters and mistresses. The network of information among the servants in London is remarkably efficient. If we wish all of the *ton* to know we are truly man and wife, and to believe that we are devoted to each other, this is the swiftest way I know to ensure that the message is delivered."

Elizabeth stared at him and he braced himself for her anger. But it did not come. Instead she spoke slowly, turning his words over in her head. "I see. You wish us to pretend to be closer than we are, so that the servants in this household will tell other servants, who will tell the ladies and gentleman in their households that it is so?"

She looked as if she were poised on the point of flight, and Thomas tried to choose his words with care. He took her hands in his. "I am concerned about what the servants will tell the other servants they know," he agreed. "But I am also thinking of us, Elizabeth. It has been twenty months since we were together. And even then we only had one night. But it was not such a very bad night, was it?"

He waited and she shook her head. Only then did he go on. "We are, for better or worse, man and wife. It seems to me we have no choice but to try to make the best of it. I told you before that I did not want nor would I settle for a bloodless marriage between us. It is time we lived like man and wife again."

Lisbeth stared at him, unable to find the words to express how she felt. She was tired and fretful and certain that the next few weeks would be distressingly uncomfortable. But Thomas was looking at her with such hope in his eyes that she could not bear to dash his spirits.

And what he had said was the truth. They could not go on forever as they were. She did not wish it any more than he did. Even now, as Thomas reached out and stroked her hair, then touched her cheek, she felt herself take a step toward him. And because that frightened her, she took a step backward.

"You are right," she said. "I know that you are. Perhaps I am simply suffering from the megrims. Too much has happened too fast for me to feel at ease with any of this. But I do want us to be man and wife again. Not just because we are bound together by wedding vows, but because I remember our wedding night, too.

Something leaped in his eyes, but he was too wise to press her further. Instead, Thomas was sympathetic, urging her to slip off her shoes and rest. He would, he promised, go downstairs and await his parents' return. No one would disturb her until it was time for dinner.

He was as good as his word, leaving the moment he saw her lie down on the bed. And only Lisbeth knew how much she wished she had the courage to ask him to stay with her instead. Not because she was afraid of his parents or what any of the servants might think, but simply because she wanted him by her side.

But she could not open her heart to him in such a way, not when he still believed her to have been unfaithful to him. It was a secret, one more secret, she would keep locked inside until she found a way to make him believe in her again, as he had once believed in the girl she had been, twenty months ago.

Chapter 10

Lisbeth was relieved to discover that the Marquess and Marchioness of Aylsham were far more civil to her than they had been thus far at any time since her marriage. And they were polite to Aunt Margaret as well. Perhaps, she told herself, it would not be such a bad thing after all, to stay here in Lord Aylsham's town house.

It was when the ladies retired to the drawing room after dinner, however, that the gloves came off. Lady Aylsham waited until they were seated and then she began her inquiry.

"How long do you and my son plan to be in London?"

"I don't know," Lisbeth admitted reluctantly. "Thomas did not say."

"I suppose you expect to be presented at court?"

Lisbeth looked to Aunt Margaret, who said calmly, "It would be customary."

Lady Aylsham turned to regard Miss Winsham with disdain. "I suppose you will also expect me to be the one to sponsor her?"

"You will most assuredly provoke unwelcome gossip if you are not," Aunt Margaret replied, not in the least cowed by the marchioness's expression.

"You will at least admit that you do not seriously expect me to pretend the boy is my grandchild!" Lady Aylsham said, a hint of desperation in her voice.

Lisbeth took a deep breath. She appeared perfectly calm. Her voice, however, was like steel. "I expect nothing of you, Lady Aylsham. Not even the simple courtesy due the wife of your son. I can understand that you might dislike me. Why should you feel otherwise? Particularly when your son married me in spite of your wishes. But what I cannot understand is your insistence that your grandchild is not Thomas's son. Why do you find it so difficult to believe?"

Now it was Lady Aylsham who drew in a deep breath. It seemed to Lisbeth that she went very pale and her voice trembled slightly as she spoke. She could not meet Lisbeth's eyes. "You forget that I have seen the child."

"Yes, and he resembles your son," Aunt Margaret interposed. "Except for the birthmark."

Lady Aylsham went even more pale. But then she seemed to come to some sort of decision. She tilted her chin upward, turned to Miss Winsham, and said, defiantly, "If you know that much, then you understand why I cannot claim him as my grandchild."

Bewildered, Lisbeth asked, "What are you talking about? Tom has no birthmark?"

"Precisely," Lady Aylsham retorted. "Every male Kepley child is born with a certain mark. It fades by the time the child is two years old, but every male Kepley is born with it. Your son was not."

"My niece has been faithful to your son," Aunt Margaret said, leaning forward.

"Without the birthmark, no one will believe it," Lady Aylsham replied.

Aunt Margaret would have argued the matter further, but Lisbeth stopped her with a wave of her hand. To Thomas's mother she said, "What sort of mark is it?"

"A dark circle at the base of the neck."

"I did not think to look for such a thing, but had it been there, I think I would have seen it," Lisbeth said slowly. She looked at the marchioness. "If this is the problem, then I understand why you refuse to believe Tom is your grandchild. And yet I know that he is your son's son. But let us be frank, Lady Aylsham. You and Lord Aylsham took me in dislike even before the child was born, long before you knew he had no such mark on him."

Again Lady Aylsham avoided meeting Lisbeth's eyes. "Do you blame us?" she asked, a trifle breathlessly. "Thomas was to have married the daughter of one of my husband's closest friends. Her family was equal to ours in both bloodlines and consequence. The two fathers planned the match when the children were in their cradles. It would have been most suitable. And he married you instead. Do you wonder that we were angry?"

Perhaps she ought to have returned a soft answer. But it was impossible. Lisbeth was far too angry for that. Without thinking, without stopping to question the wisdom of doing so, she said angrily, "Yes, I know. Lady Anna Dalwood. I also know that she was carrying a child who was not his! Did you not think it unfair to expect Thomas to tamely marry her anyway? Even knowing that presumably her affections had been given to someone else?"

Before Lady Aylsham could answer, a voice came from the doorway. "How dare you? If you know that much then you know why we asked him to do so! And have you not done the same—or worse?" the Marquess of Aylsham demanded. "For all your protestations of innocence, you cannot deny the fact that your son lacks the Kepley birthmark."

"Nonsense!" Aunt Margaret said, deciding it was once again time to intervene. "Moonshine and nonsense! Birthmark or no, Lord Thomas did father my niece's child."

Both Lisbeth and Lady Aylsham stared at her. Lady Aylsham's voice was at its frostiest as she said, "Indeed? And upon what foundation do you make such a claim?"

Miss Winsham looked at Lady Aylsham. "I know my niece. And I know enough about birthmarks to know that some may seem to run in a family and still not always be found where they are supposed to be found."

Lady Aylsham seemed flustered, then collected herself

sufficiently to peer down her patrician nose at Aunt Margaret, even though they were both the same height, particularly when seated.

"You do not know what you are talking about," she said with icy disdain.

Miss Winsham bristled. She opened her mouth for what Lisbeth knew would be a scathing reply, but Thomas forestalled her. "Enough!" Thomas said. "If I claim the child as mine, then legally he is my son. And I will not have the matter disputed by anyone else in this family."

He stared in particular at his father. The marquess stared back.

"You forget what is due this family," Lord Aylsham said.

"I forget nothing."

"You told her too much."

"I told her nothing; she overheard a great deal."

That gave the marquess pause. After a moment, he said, "You do not understand, Thomas. I suppose, however, that it will do none of us any good to have our disagreements bandied about in public. We will, in public at least, give the appearance of complacency about your marriage and the child. But do not expect us to be pleased."

Apparently Thomas knew that was the best he could hope for from his father, for he nodded. The marquess moved to sit beside his wife. Having made his decision, Lord Aylsham wasted no time.

"We had best decide," the marquess said, "how the pair of you may claim your place among the *ton* and display your apparent accord. Much as I dislike the marriage, I will allow that I should dislike even more for it to continue to be the subject of gossip."

"I suppose," Lady Aylsham said with great reluctance, "that I shall have to pay some morning calls. You had better come with me," she said to Lisbeth. "But before we do so, you will need a new wardrobe—if that dress is any example of what you have brought with you."

"This is a new gown," Lisbeth said through tightly clenched teeth. "And if the rest of my wardrobe is shabby, one might ask from what cause. One might ask through whose influence it was that I had so little access to funds, while your son was gone, that I could not dress as suits your standards."

Thomas made haste to play peacemaker. "All that is at an end now. And while the gown is new, it is scarcely in the first mode of fashion, Elizabeth. First thing tomorrow, you had best order more. You, as well, Miss Winsham, if you mean to accompany my wife about the town."

Lady Aylsham smiled and her voice was very, very sweet as she said, "Oh, there is no need for Miss Winsham to trouble herself about such things. I can accompany Elizabeth about London. Miss Winsham is free to return to her own home at any time she wishes."

Aunt Margaret snorted. "It would please you if I did, wouldn't it? As if I would be so pudding-hearted as to leave my niece friendless and unguarded in this household!"

Now it was Thomas's voice that was icy as he said, "So long as she is my wife, one can scarcely say that Elizabeth will go unguarded or friendless. Or have you decided that I am just as much her enemy as my parents?"

There were gasps of outrage from Lord and Lady Aylsham, but Aunt Margaret met Thomas's gaze steadily. "I haven't made up my mind," she said. "In any event, you aren't a woman and a woman needs a woman ally too. Which even you cannot pretend your mother would be."

He did not try to do so. Instead Thomas said, "You are, of course, always welcome to stay with us, Miss Winsham. And, indeed, I am very grateful that my wife has had you for support and assistance, these past twenty months. We merely meant that if you wished a holiday or to go and visit one of your other nieces or had something else you wished to do, that it would no longer be a hardship for Elizabeth."

The pleading look Lisbeth shot her aunt undercut Thomas's words. The older woman started to say so, then stopped herself. She understood, it seemed, that it would not help her niece if she spoke her mind. Somewhat mollified, in any event, by Thomas's words, Miss Winsham settled for a shrug of the shoulders as she replied, "Even if Elizabeth could do without me, Tom might at any moment suffer one of his attacks and I must be there to deal with it, if he does."

"Attacks?" Lord and Lady Aylsham echoed in alarm.

"What sort of attacks does your son suffer?" the marchioness asked.

"Is the condition contagious?" the marquess added with a frown.

"It is neither contagious nor alarming, not in the sense that you mean, at any rate," Thomas replied lightly, with a warning look to Lisbeth and Aunt Margaret. "The child merely suffers from difficulty in breathing, from time to time. Miss Winsham has the knack of brewing a tea that eases it for him, but she closely guards the formula of her success."

Which neatly forestalled the request that she simply hand the formula over to a nursery maid and remove the need for her presence. Both Lord and Lady Aylsham seemed to grasp that they would gain no advantage in attempting to pursue the matter and so they talked of other things.

Lady Aylsham offered advice as to the mantua maker, milliner, and glover she thought Lisbeth ought to patronize. Lord Aylsham and Thomas discussed the merits of various carriages and teams of horses, for as Thomas said bluntly, "Now that I am home and sold out my commission, I shall need to set myself up properly. I shall also need to find a riding hack for Elizabeth."

"Oh, no! That is to say, I have no need of a riding hack," Lisbeth said hastily.

"Of course you do. If my son is to bring you into fashion, and I deplore the notion but accept that it will be so, then you will want to take a turn or two in the park," the marquess said, dismissing her objections.

"I can go in the carriage."

"Far too tame," Thomas told her teasingly. "Besides, I like to ride in the park and I shall want you riding by my side, taking the shine out of all the other ladies present."

Lisbeth meant to protest, she truly did. She meant to make Thomas understand how thoroughly she disliked horses. But no one gave her a chance to do so. They all seemed to think she would be delighted with the notion. Lisbeth stared at them, her heart sinking at the thought of giving them one more reason to find her lacking.

Lady Aylsham was telling Thomas precisely the sort of gentle mare she thought every lady should have. Lord Aylsham was directing Thomas to someone looking to sell just such a creature, and at a good price. Even Aunt Margaret seemed to have deserted her cause, for she said in a low voice to Lisbeth, "This might be your chance to let go the fear you have of horses."

And so, in the end, Lisbeth did not speak. She found herself nodding as they made plans to dispose of her time while she was in London, and arranged upon whom she would call the moment she had a suitable wardrobe prepared. She listened, growing more and more unhappy with each new proposal and wishing she were back home again. But that was an empty wish and Lisbeth knew it.

She also found herself dreading the moment they would all retire for the evening and she would find herself alone in bed with Thomas for the first time since their wedding night. There was, perhaps, more than a hint of anticipation as well, but there was definitely fear.

It still felt strange to Lisbeth to have a maid to help her undress and put her to bed. To be sure, she had shared a maid with her sisters for years, but for the past twenty

months, she and Aunt Margaret had done without. So
now it was strange to have someone to help her off with
her dress and into her night shift. Someone to hang up the
gown and take care of a dozen details Lisbeth had learned
to manage herself. And yet, it was also comforting.

She found herself oddly nervous tonight, knowing that
she and Thomas would be sharing a bed. Suddenly, what
had looked so large during the day, now seemed much
smaller—too small for her to share with anyone.

But she could scarcely say so aloud. Instead she allowed herself to be undressed and then she sat at the
dressing table as she brushed out her hair. Thomas loved
her hair, loved running his fingers through it over and over
again on their wedding night. She shivered at the memory,
particularly because that wasn't all she remembered.

As if it were yesterday, Lisbeth recalled Thomas's
gentleness. The patience he had shown her and the emotions and physical feelings he had evoked in her. Would
it be like that again tonight? Or would they simply share
a bed? He had said he would not tolerate a bloodless marriage. He had told her that he wanted to be man and wife
again. But did he mean tonight? And, perhaps more important, did she want him to mean tonight?

Lisbeth let herself be tucked into the bed, a candle on
the nightstand. She tried to decide whether to sit up and
try to read a book while she waited for Thomas, or
whether she ought to simply go to sleep. In the end she
clutched the locket in her hand and let her thoughts run
riot instead.

Why hadn't he told her what he wished? Why hadn't
he told her what he intended? And why hadn't Aunt Margaret told her about the birthmark? It would have made
Thomas's suspicions a great deal easier to tolerate if she
had known.

But it was all of a piece, Lisbeth told herself irritably.
No one told her anything. Thomas did as he chose and
then informed her of his wishes afterward. He did not ask

what hers might be. And why should he? He was her husband. By law, he did not need to do anything else.

But, a tiny voice whispered at the back of her mind, she had hoped that he would. She had hoped that the promise of their wedding night would be played out in the discovery that Thomas was as concerned with pleasing her out of bed as he had been with pleasing her in it.

In her heart, Lisbeth had hoped she would discover Thomas to be so different from her father that she need never fear her feelings would be run over roughshod ever again. She should have known that was the wishful thinking of a child! She should have remembered that Thomas was simply a man, and men always did what they wished.

Given the direction of her thoughts, it was perhaps not surprising that when Thomas finally came to bed, Lisbeth was not precisely in a mood to welcome him.

"There you are," she grumbled, pulling away when he would have reached for her.

"Have you been waiting impatiently for me?" he asked with perfect amiability, reaching for her again.

She pulled even farther away. "I have been impatient with you, would be more precise to say," she countered. "Where have you been, Thomas?"

"Talking with my father. Why? Is something amiss?"

She didn't mean to be missish, truly she didn't. Lisbeth had meant to remain dignified and calm, but somehow her voice didn't sound that way at all as she replied, "Everything!"

"Indeed?"

Was he angry? He sounded, at the very least, to be annoyed. Well, so too was she annoyed, and it was past time that she told him so!

Lisbeth sat up and confronted Thomas directly. "Why didn't you tell me about the birthmark?"

"I hoped you would tell me the truth of your own accord," he answered gently. "I hoped you would tell me because you trusted me and not because you knew I had proof."

She stared at Thomas. It was hopeless. He truly believed that Tom was not his son and while he was wrong, at least now she understood why. She tried another approach.

"You brought us to London," Lisbeth said, with some asperity. "Which is all very well, but you also decided we must live in the same household as your parents without even asking me. Knowing they cannot abide me and that they believe I have been unfaithful to you. You even insist that we share one bed and then you take forever to come to it."

Her voice faltered on these last few words and Kepley smiled. "I am here now," he said, reaching out to stroke her shoulder.

Lisbeth shivered and tried to pull away. "I no longer care!"

"No?"

His voice was as soft as a caress, and as he spoke he twisted a strand of hair around his fingers, sending more shivers up her back. He kissed the base of her neck and it took away her breath. He kissed her shoulder and then ran a finger down the center of her back, something she could not possibly ignore.

She didn't want him to touch her, Lisbeth told herself. She didn't want him to make her feel this way. And so she would tell him. But when she spoke, her voice did not sound very much like itself.

"Stop!" was scarcely more than a whisper.

"Do you really want me to do so?" he asked, his hands continuing to remind her of all that she was asking to give up.

Thomas leaned over her so that she could not evade his gaze. He was smiling but his eyes were serious, demanding honesty. And it was honesty that Lisbeth found she could not deny him.

"I don't know what I wish," she confessed. "When you touch me like this my senses are all disarrayed. I like it, and yet I cannot help but feel it keeps us from talking about the things that matter."

"This," he said, kissing her, "is what matters. And this," he added, touching the creamy skin at her throat at the neckline of her night shift.

Suddenly Lisbeth found she no longer wished to argue. Tomorrow, she told herself. Tomorrow there would be sufficient time to discuss everything with Thomas. Tomorrow would be sufficient time to hold him to account. For now, she gave herself over to pleasure.

Chapter 11

Lisbeth woke with a start. She was not accustomed to finding anyone in her bed in the morning. But Thomas lay beside her, still asleep, with one arm thrown over her. And in sleep, his face seemed so peaceful that she found herself wishing it could always be this way between them.

He stirred then, as though sensing her scrutiny. She could see the moment Thomas realized he wasn't alone in the bed because a smile crossed his face. She kissed him, and his arm came around her in a viselike grip. Lisbeth found she rather liked the sensation and snuggled closer. Slowly he opened his eyes.

"I have not woken to so pleasant a sight in twenty months," Thomas said.

He pulled her half onto him and his hand began stroking lazy circles on her back. Lisbeth found it hard to catch her breath to answer him.

"Let us begin anew, here and now, Elizabeth," he told her, his hands making it more and more difficult for her to think. "Tell me who Tom's father is and we shall never speak of it again."

It was as if she had been doused with cold water. Lisbeth rolled off of Thomas and glared at him. "*You* are the father!" she said.

He gave an exasperated snort of disgust and threw the covers back. Then he got out of bed and rose to his feet. "I have told you I will forgive you, however it came about," Thomas said, his voice low and angry. "But I will not tolerate being lied to."

He waited and Lisbeth could only stare at him. What was there to say that she had not said before? He waited and in the end he turned and strode away from her, anger in every line of his body. Lisbeth felt all the warmth of the night before slipping away from her.

"Where are you going, Thomas?" she asked, unable to stop herself.

He turned and looked at her. She expected the anger. She would not have been surprised if he had looked at her with icy disdain. But suddenly she could see only sadness and hurt in his eyes, and somehow that made everything worse.

Abruptly he came back over to the bed. Almost as though it were against his will, he bent down and stroked her hair. Lisbeth could see the way Thomas tried to keep his voice gentle as he said, "Never mind, Elizabeth. I cannot force you to trust me if you are not ready to do so, and I am wrong to try. Rest awhile longer, if you wish. I am going to get dressed, and then I am going out. I will be back later."

Lisbeth didn't want to let him go. She caught his hand in hers. "Where are you going?" she asked again.

There was sadness and pain and something more that tugged at her heart as he said, "I don't know."

And then, before she could even think what else to say to Thomas, he pulled his hand free and turned his back on her. A few moments later, Lisbeth could hear him moving about in the dressing room next to the bedroom, but she knew better than to try to follow him there. Slowly she got out of bed. She didn't bother to ring for the maid to help her dress. She had long ago adapted the fastenings of all her gowns to make it possible for her to manage for herself.

Her hands faltered for a moment. Gowns. She was supposed to go order new gowns today. It wasn't that she disliked the notion, for she didn't. It would, she thought, be something of a treat not to have to cut and sew her clothes herself. And there was a part of her that had long wished for the chance to have the sort of clothing that other ladies could afford.

But it also reminded her of her secret. Last night the marquess and marchioness had talked again of consequence and bloodlines. What would they say, she wondered, if they knew she had been little better than a seamstress these past many months? It wasn't really a question, for she knew the answer all too well. It would be one more reason to despise her. Lisbeth could only hope they would never find out.

Downstairs, Thomas told a startled butler that he was going out and had no notion when he would return. "But, sir, what am I to tell the marquess and marchioness?"

"I don't know!" Thomas said shortly. Then, realizing it was unfair to take his foul mood out on this poor fellow, he added, "It is time, indeed past time, that I renewed old acquaintances in the city. I have no notion whom I may meet or what plans we may make."

The butler's tension eased at that. He smiled indulgently and replied, "Yes, of course, sir. I shall tell them. And may I venture to say that I think they will be pleased to see you getting out and about?"

Thomas grinned. "You may say anything you please, to anyone you wish," he said impishly, "so long as I need not be there to hear the wrath if you are taken as speaking out of turn."

The butler did not laugh, of course, but it seemed to Thomas that he came very close. And that cheered his spirits. His good humor lasted, however, only until he remembered Lisbeth. What was the truth? he wondered. He wanted to believe her when she said she had been faithful, but there was the evidence of Tom, without the Kepley birthmark, to prove her a liar.

Or had she been attacked? Had she been taken against her will, perhaps? And was she now afraid to confide in him? That thought was even worse than the first and Thomas devoutly hoped it was not so.

Surely it was because he was so preoccupied that when he abruptly changed direction Thomas nearly collided with someone. He apologized profusely, but as he did so, a movement caught his attention. It was as if someone had hastily stepped into a doorway for fear of being seen.

Thomas shook his head. It was nonsense! Who, here in London, would behave in such a way? He continued down the street, but now his senses were alert, perhaps too alert, for he could have sworn there was something familiar about one of the beggars on the street. The fellow had a scruffy look about him and his clothes were ragged and filthy. He was not by any means the sort of man Thomas would have known.

Perhaps he was a fellow soldier? So many of the men who had returned from the war had been unable to find employment. Perhaps he was one of the men Kepley had, at one time or another, under his command? Or perhaps he was a fellow prisoner of war or even someone injured at the same time he had been.

That thought caused Thomas to move toward the man, meaning to speak with him. He knew he was fortunate in having an income and estate waiting upon his return to England. Many, perhaps most, returning soldiers were not so fortunate. If he was indeed someone Thomas had known, he meant to help the fellow, if he could.

But something about Thomas seemed to frighten the fellow and he turned and moved away as fast as he could—faster than Thomas could follow without causing his leg to ache abominably. It was as the fellow turned a corner that Thomas suddenly realized who the man reminded him of and he started to run, oblivious to the discomfort in his leg.

He was not fast enough. By the time he reached the corner, the other man was nowhere to be seen. Thomas ground his teeth in frustration. The beggar could not possibly, he told himself firmly, have been Jean Merlion. There was no reason for him to be in England. Surely the Frenchman would never have taken such a risk.

But as much as he tried to be reasonable, Thomas could not shake the feeling that the man on the street had indeed been Merlion. It was therefore in a far more sober frame of mind, that Thomas continued on his way.

London, on a late spring morning, could seem almost beautiful. It lacked the dark haze of coal smoke that hung over the city for most of the winter, but did not yet have the malodorous scent that seemed everywhere in summer. The sun was bright, but not so bright that a lady need fear damage to her delicate complexion. It was a day to be outside, not indoors with a mantua maker. But that was where Lisbeth and Miss Winsham found themselves.

Lisbeth was very well aware her wardrobe fell sadly short of what a lady would need to cut a dash in the city. And indeed, she was looking forward to indulging herself. More than that, she was looking forward to the moment when Thomas would see her in her new finery and admire her the way he once had done, so many months ago. After last night, it was suddenly of the utmost importance to her that he approve of the woman she had become.

Why had no one ever told her, Lisbeth asked herself, how wonderful it could be between a woman and a man? Why had Aunt Margaret only spoken of duty and submitting to her husband's wishes, and said nothing of pleasure? Well, at least now she knew why housemaids giggled as they made plans to meet footmen in deserted corridors! To be sure, she had known since her wedding night. But last night had been a very pleasant reminder.

"What the devil are you thinking?" Miss Winsham demanded, frowning at her niece. "You look indecently pleased with yourself this morning!"

Lisbeth flushed but grinned unrepentantly at her aunt. "You don't wish to know," she said primly. "And, in any event, we are here."

Miss Winsham grumbled all the way into the establishment, but she began to unbend when the staff greeted them both with kind attention. At the magic words, "an entire new wardrobe," Madame Salvage herself was instantly summoned to supervise all the discussions with Lisbeth and her aunt. And when she learned that Miss Winsham also wished to commission a few gowns, her affability knew no bounds. Tea was brought for the ladies, they were taken to the most comfortable chamber, and a spirited discussion of the styles and fabrics and colors that would best suit each of the ladies then ensued.

By the time Lisbeth and Miss Winsham left, some three hours later, all three were dizzy with delight. For Lisbeth and her aunt, it was the prospect of beautiful clothes again after such a long time of scrimping and saving. For the mantua maker, it was the prospect of the largest commission she had yet enjoyed that year. Nor did she discount the usefulness of dressing a lady who would show off her creations to such advantage. That, itself, would mean an increase in commissions to offset the slight discount she had offered the ladies when she realized they meant to stick to a budget.

Indeed, Lisbeth was already beginning to feel some pangs of conscience over the amount she had just spent. Miss Winsham dismissed her concerns with a snort of impatience.

"You are merely making up for lost time, and whose fault, may I ask, is it that you need do so at all? Kepley owes you this much and far more! When the bills come, hand them over to him. And if he cuts up stiff, ask him if he wishes his wife to dress in rags! He has already told you he does not, and I see no reason to disbelieve him."

Lisbeth could find no reason to disagree. Instead, she looked at her aunt and said, "Need we go directly back? Or do you think we dare indulge in further extravagance?"

Something seemed to twinkle in Miss Winsham's eyes. "Of course we dare!" she retorted. "Recollect that you were told to rig yourself out in style. That means hats, reticules, gloves, slippers, and stockings, and all manner of things, including fans and shawls. I know just where to find them."

And she did. It was astonishing to Lisbeth that her aunt, who had spent so little time in London, always seemed to know precisely where the best things were to be found. She also knew how much to pay and when a price could be reduced or when it would stand firm. She knew who made the finest gloves and which merchant had the cheapest but still very nice ribbons. She even knew where they could go for ices to revive their flagging spirits.

To be sure, Lisbeth had had a Season in London herself and then spent time there after her eldest sister was married to Sir Robert Stamford. So she would not have been entirely lost on her own. But her knowledge of London was as nothing compared to Aunt Margaret's.

It was sheer luxury, Lisbeth thought, to be able to indulge in the fantasy that she and Miss Winsham were like every other lady in London. They were not, however. As they were about to leave the shop that sold ices and bakery treats, a girl came out of the back with a tray of tarts to put on the counter. Suddenly she stumbled and the tray of tarts crashed to the floor. Instantly the man running the shop turned and started to shout at the girl.

"Clumsy fool! Pick them up! Every one! You'll have a

beating for this, you will! It's the third time this week. You'll regret your clumsiness, you will."

Aunt Margaret did not hesitate. She marched over to the counter, opened her reticule, and put several coins on the counter, drawing the shopkeeper's attention.

"That ought to pay for the damaged tarts," Miss Winsham said briskly.

The shopkeeper gaped at her. "Why should you pay for 'er clumsiness?" he demanded. Then, as though realizing his folly, he hastily added, "It's very kind of you and welcome and of course I'll go easier on the girl 'cause you did."

Miss Winsham nodded. "Yes, you will, because she is coming with me."

The shopkeeper gaped even more. Then a cunning look came into his eyes. "Coming wif you? But I needs 'er 'ere."

"No, you don't," Lisbeth said firmly. "She will cost you far too much in damaged goods."

"But I've paid for 'er, I 'ave. Good money to 'ave 'er as me assistant."

"And we shall pay you good money to let her come with us," Miss Winsham replied as she placed still more coins on the counter. Then, before he could object, she said to the girl, who was also staring at them, "Come along! We haven't all day! It is time to go!"

"But what will you do wif 'er?" the shopkeeper asked.

Miss Winsham stared at him. "I hardly," she said in her haughtiest voice, "believe that is your concern."

And then Aunt Margaret swept out of the shop. Lisbeth and the girl hastily followed. Behind them, Lisbeth could hear patrons of the shop exclaiming in disapproval at the eccentric behavior.

"Did you see that?"

"Scandalous, that's what it is. Scandalous! A good beating; that's what all these girls need."

"What on earth is she doing, concerning herself with a shop girl?"

"Perhaps she was once a shop girl herself. If so, one can guess how she rose from that position!"

This last comment was accompanied by snickers and Lisbeth was glad the door had closed behind them and they could hear no more. Outside, she and Aunt Margaret looked at each other and then at the girl, who looked both fearful and hopeful.

"What is your name?" Lisbeth asked.

"Hope, ma'am. Thank you, ma'am, for paying for the tarts," she added, looking at Miss Winsham. "But ma'am, what do you mean to do with me?"

"That, Hope, depends on you," Aunt Margaret replied briskly. "For the moment, we are going to get in that waiting carriage and go to a place I know. There are a number of people who will be very happy to help you find a new position."

Hope started to back away, shaking her head vigorously as she did so. "Oh, no, ma'am. I've 'eard about ladies like you. And them sorts of 'ouses. I'm not going to one of them. I'm not!"

She would have run if Lisbeth and Aunt Margaret had not each taken one arm and held her. Another lady might have been bewildered by the girl's fears, but Aunt Margaret knew and had told Lisbeth about the conditions in which far too many young girls found themselves.

So now Lisbeth said soothingly, "No, no, not that sort of house, Hope. You quite mistake the matter! My aunt means that she has friends who can help you find a position as a seamstress or a kitchen maid or a shop girl in a different sort of shop or a nursemaid or almost any sort of work you wish."

Hope stopped struggling. "Truly?" she asked Miss Winsham, the suspicion evident in her voice.

"It is just as my niece has said," Aunt Margaret confirmed. "I assure you, the last place on earth that I would take you is a brothel. I rescue girls from such places. I do not put them there."

Hope had no reason to trust Lisbeth or Miss Winsham. But she must have seen something in their faces that persuaded her, for suddenly she nodded and climbed into the waiting carriage. Aunt Margaret paused to give the coachman the necessary directions and a minute later they were off.

Inside the carriage, Lisbeth smiled reassuringly at Hope and then spoke to Aunt Margaret. "You have been missing your friends, haven't you?"

"Yes. And I had meant to go there today anyway, but I had not meant to drag you along, Elizabeth."

"I don't mind."

"I mind for you. Kepley won't like it," Miss Winsham warned her niece.

Lisbeth tilted up her chin. "I don't care. Besides, I have been curious to see this place and meet your friends, and this will give me the chance."

From the seat opposite Lisbeth and Miss Winsham, Hope asked, "Why? Why do you wish to help me?"

Aunt Margaret stared back at the girl. Lisbeth would dearly have liked to hear the answer, but the older woman merely replied, "Doesn't matter. Just be grateful I am."

And that put an end to further conversation. Fortunately, it was not very far to their destination and a short time later the three women were shown into a parlor crowded with an assortment of people, all very busy discussing plans and people and things to be done. At the sight of Miss Winsham and her two companions, however, all activity ceased and there was a general rush to welcome her.

"Miss Winsham! How are you!"

"It has been far too long!"

"How long do you mean to be in London?"

"Who are these two?"

This last question caused Aunt Margaret to draw a

deep breath and step back. "This is my niece, Lady Thomas Kepley. And this is Hope. We have just rescued her from a shop and she needs a place to stay until a new position can be found for her."

It was, Lisbeth thought with some amusement, a measure of how different the priorities of this house were from those of the *ton* that attention swirled around Hope instead of her. Very shortly one of the older women had drawn the shop girl to her side and was deep in conversation with her. Only when the two left the room did attention turn back to Aunt Margaret. Lisbeth still found herself essentially ignored and felt rather pleased that rank had no influence with these people, only actions.

As for Miss Winsham, it felt good, very good, to be back, doing what she was meant to do. Even to herself, until now, Margaret had not allowed herself to admit how much she had missed her friends and how much she had missed the satisfaction of rescuing girls and boys like Hope. Now that she had come here today, she was not, Miss Winsham knew, going to be able to stay away.

By the time they arrived home, the carriage was heaped with packages, and many more had been sent directly to the Marquess of Aylsham's town house. It should not, therefore, have come as a surprise to anyone as to where they had been. Which is perhaps why Lisbeth was so unprepared to find Thomas waiting for her in their bedroom, pacing the floor with unmistakable anxiety.

"Where have you been?" he demanded the moment he saw his wife.

Lisbeth stared at him, bewildered. "You told me to go refurbish my wardrobe. I have done so. I have commissioned all the gowns your mother insisted I would need, and Aunt Margaret and I sought out the necessaries to go with them."

Thomas fought for self-control. How could he tell her

the reason for his worry? He knew it was most unlikely that Jean Merlion had followed him here from France. But absurd or not, he could not shake the fear. And how could he explain that if he had, the man might try to hurt her?

It was fear for her safety that made Thomas speak more sharply to Elizabeth than he had intended. "You ought to have been back hours ago!"

He could see an angry flush in her cheeks, but she merely laughed. "Indeed?" she replied in too bright a voice. "If you can say so, then it is evident you have no notion of what shopping for a lady's things requires. No, nor any sense of how dictatorial a mantua maker may be. Argue with Madame Salvage, if you please, and not with me, as to how long is needed to choose a wardrobe."

He stepped back and fell silent. Thomas knew his anger made no sense and was unfair to her. But knowing so did not change how he felt. So rather than stay and lash out at her again, he turned on his heel and left the room.

Behind him, Lisbeth stared after her husband in bewilderment. She had won that encounter, she thought. But she felt neither pleasure nor triumph. Indeed, she had the impulse to reach out and stop him. But she didn't, and then it was too late. She could hear the front door open and close as he left the house.

Outside, Thomas began to walk briskly, his face set in a scowl. He had good reason, he told himself firmly, to be upset with Elizabeth. It was not that he wished or meant to be a dictatorial husband, but he *was* her husband! She ought to realize he had only her welfare at heart. She ought to understand that it was his responsibility to make certain she was safe.

Thomas could not recall his mother ever speaking to his father as Elizabeth had just spoken to him. Nor could he recall hearing any ladies of his acquaintance speaking in such a manner to any of their husbands.

A small voice nagged at him that perhaps it was because most wives would do so only in private and that perhaps more of this went on than he knew. But he didn't want to think about it; he wanted to hold on to his anger. Because if he was angry, then he wouldn't have to remember how afraid he had been that something had happened to her. He didn't have to remember wondering how he would go on if something had happened to her.

Better to be angry. Better to set strict rules for the future. Better to go and see his friends. And then, with one or two in tow, he would go and buy some horses. He might not know ladies clothing, but he certainly knew how to judge horseflesh to a nicety!

And if he bought Elizabeth a riding mare and a gelding for himself, then they could go riding in the park every morning, and surely that would give a different direction to her thoughts. Surely, while they were out riding, he could begin to bring her to a recognition of what she owed him as her husband, and how she ought to conduct herself while she was in London. That she had managed just fine while he was gone was a truth he preferred to ignore.

Besides, Elizabeth had not managed her conduct just fine, Thomas told himself. She had a child who was not his and rumors abounded, making it imperative that they do what they could to retrieve her reputation as soon as possible. No, Elizabeth needed his guidance and counsel, even if she did not wish to acknowledge that truth just yet.

That put Thomas in a more cheerful frame of mind. So much so that when he encountered Sir Robert, Elizabeth's oldest sister's husband, on the street, he greeted him with perfect amiability.

"Hallo, Stamford! How do you go on? How are your wife and daughter? And the baby?"

Stamford grinned. "My wife is fine, though both my children are driving her to distraction. But how do you go on? I was never more happy than when I heard you had survived and found your way back to England!"

At these words, Thomas frowned. He lowered his voice slightly and said, "Yes, well, I do not wish to make every one on the street a present of my experiences. Suffice it to say that I was as happy to be back home as you were to hear that I was."

Stamford cocked his head to the side and Thomas had the impression that he saw and understood far more than one might wish. After a moment, he nodded and said, "Call on me tomorrow, at my town house. We may be private there and you can tell me the whole story."

Thomas stiffened. This was not what he wished! "I . . . er . . . That is to say, I cannot. I . . . er . . . have a previous engagement."

"Like that, is it?" Stamford said with a frown. "When will you be free to speak? Or are you bound to secrecy forever? No, forget I asked. No doubt you are under orders to pretend that nothing has happened at all, except, of course, whatever the official story might be. Very well. Come and see me when you are free to speak. I shall enjoy hearing the tale. But for now I will cease to press you. Good day, Kepley. Give my love to your wife and tell her that if she does not come to call soon, Alexandra will descend upon her without warning and read her a royal scold!"

In spite of himself, Thomas managed a shaky laugh. "I shall tell her. And if your wife is anything like mine, I shall advise Elizabeth to be very careful not to offend her."

Stamford laughed and the two men moved away from each other. It took great resolution, but Thomas did not look over his shoulder to see if the fellow was watching him.

How the devil did Stamford know, or, more likely guess so much? And who else was likely to do so? Thomas could only hope that Stamford's discretion was to be depended upon! Perhaps he should urge Elizabeth to visit her sister. Perhaps he ought to take her there himself. He could speak with Stamford and discover the extent of his knowledge.

Abruptly Thomas shook his head. The war was over and he was home. What difference did it make what Stamford knew or thought he knew? His interest ought to be his wife and family now, and his most pressing concern nothing more than a visit to Tattersall's.

His mind made up, Thomas was pleased to encounter friends at that establishment and even more pleased when he spied the perfect mounts, both for himself and for his wife.

Chapter 12

L isbeth knew that if she did not go see her sisters they would come in search of her. That was why she was perfectly happy to set out with Aunt Margaret and Thomas to see them the next day. To be sure, she had been somewhat surprised that he had suggested doing so, but she was certainly not going to object.

Her sisters, however, were before her. Even as she was coming down the stairs to leave the marquess's town house, her sisters were admitted at the front door. With a crow of delight, she flew down the last few steps to greet them.

"Tessa! Alex! How are you? You look wonderful! Come upstairs and tell me how you have been!"

The Aylsham's butler looked on with approval at this display of sisterly affection. Thomas smiled, greeted her sisters, and then quietly slipped away. Aunt Margaret looked over each of her nieces with a critical eye and then admitted, "Marriage seems to suit you both very well."

Tessa and Alex looked at each other and laughed. "We think so," they agreed.

Then they looked carefully, perhaps too carefully, at Lisbeth and Aunt Margaret. Before they could say something in front of the servants, Lisbeth turned and started up the stairs. "There is a parlor up here where we might be perfectly private," she said in her gayest voice.

"After we see the nursery!" Tessa announced.

"Yes, we've yet to see Tom, and that must come first!" Alex agreed.

"Go with Elizabeth," Aunt Margaret said. "I shall go up and have the nursery maid bring him down to the parlor. There is no point in setting up the backs of the nursery staff by invading their territory."

Since it was not a point any of the sisters could very well dispute, too well aware of how their own nursery staff would feel, they went with good grace to the parlor where Margaret soon appeared with a nursery maid and Tom in tow. Tessa and Alex exclaimed over the child, vied to have him sit in their laps, and generally paid him a great deal of attention. By the time they were ready to let him go, he was quite exhausted, enough to be ready to take a nap. Or so, the nursery maid proclaimed darkly, she hoped!

When they were once again alone, Tessa and Alex looked at Lisbeth and Aunt Margaret. Then they looked at each other, and by silent agreement, Alex spoke first.

"You have fobbed us off for the past twenty months, Lisbeth. We have only seen you a couple of times, for the briefest of visits, since you moved to Kepley's estate, a few months after you married and he was, as we supposed, killed. We respected your privacy—partly because we understood, and partly because we were each preoccupied with the exigencies of having babies ourselves. But no more. We want to know precisely what has taken place since you last allowed us to see you! And Aunt Margaret, we hold you to blame for not keeping us better informed."

Miss Winsham flushed, but stood her ground. Lisbeth hesitated. "I did not want you to worry," she said.

Tessa snorted a most unladylike snort. "We did so anyway!" she said.

Lisbeth met her sister's eyes frankly. "Not as much as you would have worried if I had told you the truth."

She did so, then, omitting very little. Now that Thomas

was home, and her circumstances altered, the time for secrecy was past. It was evident, however, that it would take Alex and Tessa some time to forgive her for deceiving them.

When she was done, Alex looked again at Aunt Margaret. "I blame you," she repeated, "for not telling us!"

"I told her not to," Lisbeth protested.

"She should have done so anyway!" Tessa exclaimed, a tear trickling down her cheek. "I cannot bear to think what you have gone through!"

Miss Winsham regarded her nieces with a grim expression on her face. "To what end should I have told you how matters stood?" she demanded in icy accents. "So you could demand that Elizabeth come stay with either of you? She would not have done so."

"We could have sent her funds!" Tessa protested.

"Not enough to matter."

"We should have known," Alex persisted. "We would have tried to do something!"

Lisbeth reached out a hand to each of her sisters. "It was not so very bad," she told them firmly. "It sounds far worse in the telling! Look, we did not have funds when we lived at home, before Papa died, and we still managed. That experience stood me in good stead, I can tell you! With a young baby, I had no wish to gad about anyway. And I truly did not want you to worry."

Neither Alex nor Tessa looked convinced. And when Kepley chose that moment to rap on the parlor door and ask to join them, he was greeted with glares of outrage. Thomas looked to Lisbeth. She could easily read the unspoken question in his comical expression.

"They blame you for having your ship sink and being captured by the French," she said smoothly.

"We do not!" Alex retorted indignantly.

"But we do blame you, sir, for not making sufficient provision for your wife before you left," Tessa added, with great dignity.

Stung, Thomas said, "I did make provision. How could I know someone would intervene and overturn all my arrangements? You cannot think I would have wanted Elizabeth to find herself in the situation that she did! Or that I wished to find myself where I was."

Soothingly, Alex replied, "No, of course not! It is just that we care a great deal for our sister and now that we have found out how precarious her situation was, our emotions are running rather high."

Thomas looked at Lisbeth. "You didn't tell them?" he asked incredulously. "You did not go to visit and they did not come to visit you?"

She flushed, but then her chin came up in an unconscious gesture of defiance. "I visited them, but I took care that they would not know. I did not want their pity."

"Yes, but you could have had their comfort and support!" he retorted.

"Yes, Lisbeth, you could have had our comfort and support," Tessa echoed dutifully, her eyes dancing with both anger and laughter.

Lisbeth gritted her teeth. "I did not think, sir, that you would wish our affairs bandied about. I did not think you would wish the world to know the conditions under which I struggled. Was I mistaken?"

It was his turn to flush. "This was not the whole world," Thomas said, his voice pitched low. "These are your sisters! And, yes, I think I should have preferred to have them know your circumstances, than to have had you go through it by yourself. Do you think I like the notion that I could not be there to support you? Do you think I like the notion that you were in such straits and alone?"

Aunt Margaret cleared her throat pointedly. "She was not alone, sir. She had me."

"Oh, for—" Thomas bit back the oath he had been about to utter. Instead he ran a hand through his hair and said, "Yes, yes, I know you were there, Miss Winsham.

And I do not discount the importance of your support—
or your healing skills with her son. But I simply wish
Elizabeth had availed herself of all the possible support
and assistance open to her!"

Alex and Tessa heard precisely what he said. As one,
they turned to Lisbeth. Very carefully Alex said, "Did you
leave something out, Sister?"

"How have Aunt Margaret's healing skills been important to your son?" Tessa added, leaning forward.

So Lisbeth told them. It was not that she had meant to
keep it from them, and so she said. It was simply that she
thought there had been enough for them to absorb as it
was. But now she told them everything, including the
predictions of the physicians she had consulted, and
about Dr. Brooks, who had at least listened to Aunt Margaret and admitted to her skills.

Alex and Tessa were still not pleased, but at least they
understood. To Lisbeth's surprise, Alex even found the
name Brooks familiar.

"I think he once visited Henley Hall," she said. "It was
when Mama was very ill, not long before she died."

Aunt Margaret shook her head. "So he said, but I do
not remember such a visit," she said impatiently.

Alex frowned, trying to recall that time, so many years
earlier. "I think you must have gone somewhere, Aunt
Margaret," she said slowly. "I remember Mama calling
for you and Papa saying that the—forgive me—*blasted
gypsy* was not anywhere to be found."

Miss Winsham smiled grimly. "Yes, your father used
to call me that quite often. He could not forgive me for
going to live in my cottage in the woods and refusing all
his attempts to make a match for me. Never mind that I
knew he always did so to his own advantage. Lord Henley could not forgive me for wishing to live my life as I
chose, and in such an unconventional way."

It was Tessa who said, "Yes, that's all very well, but
what are we to do about your son, Tom, Lisbeth?"

"Do about Tom?" Thomas asked, taken aback.

"Should we try to find another physician, one who might have some better notions?" Tessa persisted.

"I have written to the best men in London," Lisbeth said quietly. "Not one of them offered me any hope."

"We must simply try harder," Alex said firmly. She looked at Kepley. "Surely, now that you are home, you must have some notions, sir."

Thomas rose to his feet. He would not discuss the child with his wife's sisters. It was a pity, of course, about the boy's ill health, but surely they could not expect him to feel what he would if it were his own son?

He could feel their puzzled stares upon his back, but he could not answer them. It was Lisbeth who did so. In a voice entirely devoid of emotion she told them, "My husband does not believe that Tom is his son. He thinks, you see, that I played him false."

And that drew down upon Thomas's head every opprobrium open to a lady to speak! Thomas found himself hard-pressed to know what to say or do. Finally, when they drew breath and paused, he hastily said to Lisbeth, "Before you allow this to go any further, tell them why I am so certain this is not my son! Tell them that he lacks the birthmark that is the heritage of every male child in my family for a great many generations past! And then allow them to berate me if you will."

In the stunned silence that followed this pronouncement, Thomas hastily made good his escape. Behind him, he knew the silence would not last for long. He also had a very strong notion that they would not take as seriously as he did the lack of the birthmark. These were Elizabeth's sisters, so naturally they were bound to take her side.

In their place, it was what Thomas, himself, would have done. But as much as he understood, he would not stay and allow himself to be abused. Not when he knew that he, at least, had always acted in good faith. Not when he knew that he had offered Elizabeth understanding, if she would only tell him the truth! Besides, this was as good a time as any to call upon Stamford to discover how much he knew and just how far the breach of security had spread.

Back in the parlor, he was quite correct to assume they were speaking indignantly on Lisbeth's behalf.

"How dare Kepley accuse you of such a thing?" Tessa demanded.

"We know you wouldn't have played him false," Alex added stoutly.

"I still say there is something havey-cavey about this supposed birthmark," Aunt Margaret added grimly.

Lisbeth tried to stem the tide of indignation. However angry she might at times feel with Thomas, she did not wish to hear him spoken of in such a way by anyone else. So now she held the locket tight and felt it grow warm in her grasp.

"He believes what he believes," she said. "And to be fair, he has told me that if I had played him false, he would understand because he knows I thought him dead. He has offered to raise Tom just as if he were his own son. Which, of course, he is!" she added hastily. "But you see, I do understand why he would have such doubts—if there is such a family birthmark. I cannot explain why Tom does not show such a mark, but I can understand why it would give Thomas and his parents pause. How could they not wonder at its absence?"

"Very easily!" Alex retorted tartly. "They might put faith in you, rather than in some absurd family legend. They might look at Tom, really look at him. How could they miss the way his eyes match Kepley's? How could they mistake that smile as belonging to anyone else but a child of his?"

"And even if he had his doubts, he ought not to have spoken them aloud to you!" Tessa added stoutly. "I still say you ought to come stay with one of us."

Lisbeth shook her head. "I know there have been ru-mors. How much worse do you think they would be if I did as you suggest? No, I must stay here, with Thomas. He has promised we shall do whatever is necessary to put paid to all the vile tales that have been told. He has even said he means to publicly make much of Tom—as though he does believe he is his son. And though of course I wish he did believe me, that kindness does much to touch my heart."

It was, both Tessa and Alex had to allow, a handsome gesture, given the state of Kepley's own emotions. It did much to reconcile them to the choice their sister had made. Still, both ladies were extremely thoughtful, a short time later, as they left the house. Lisbeth could only hope their bemused expressions were not going to lead to behavior she was going to regret!

Meanwhile, perhaps she ought to go in search of Thomas. He had not looked pleased when he left the parlor. But then, he ought not to have intruded on their tête-à-tête.

Unfortunately, Thomas was nowhere to be found. In the end, Lisbeth settled for finding Aunt Margaret and making plans for which park they would take Tom to for his afternoon airing. Not that the nursery maid was going to be pleased to have her authority usurped this way, but Lisbeth and Aunt Margaret and Tom had grown accus-tomed to spending their afternoons together out-of-doors. And even though they were in London, she meant to continue that tradition.

Stamford did not seem surprised to see Lord Thomas show up at his door. When they were alone in his library, he grinned at the other man and said, "Come to escape the ladies, have you? They can be a tad overwhelming at times!"

In spite of himself, Thomas smiled in return. "They were about to rip my character to shreds, and I thought it prudent to remove myself beforehand."

Stamford nodded. For a long moment the two men stared at each other and then Thomas sighed. He had neither time nor patience for delicacy. He was going to have to be blunt. "Yesterday you seemed to imply you knew what my circumstances had been these past twenty months," he said carefully. "Will you tell me just what it is you heard?"

In reply, Stamford leaned forward so that he could pitch his voice low enough that even someone with an ear pressed to the door of the library could not have overheard what he had to say. It was a discretion for which Thomas was grateful.

"I have sources, discreet sources, you will understand. They knew that I might feel some concern when you were, as it seemed, lost at sea. A couple of months ago, long after we all gave you up for dead, word reached me that you were alive. I was told that you had been captured but managed to escape. I was also told that you had managed to get word back to our lines with information invaluable to Wellington—and that you were staying behind the lines as long as you were needed, to collect more such information. I was told not to expect you before the war ended. And I was warned not to tell anyone, not even your wife, that I knew you were still alive. I collect the French thought you had been killed in one encounter or another and both your safety and your effectiveness might depend on no one knowing the truth."

Thomas drew in a deep breath of dismay. His superiors would not be happy to hear that anyone had heard anything. Stamford seemed to understand his concern for he added, "Believe me, my sources were highly placed and I would not have been told if they had not been absolutely certain I was to be trusted. So far as I know, Rivendale is the only other person of your acquaintance who was told. And he is to be trusted as well. From your silence, I presume the information was accurate. What I do not understand is your dismay. Surely now that the war is over it cannot matter? Who is to care what happened?"

"One hopes that it is over," Thomas replied. "But there are reasons to believe that not everyone is willing to accept the victory. And should we ever need to use the same methods again that we used when I was in France, we should prefer that no one know precisely what it was we did or how we did it."

Stamford nodded. "Yes, I see. And you may be sure I shall not speak of it. I only did so because, well, if it were true, it occurred to me that you might find yourself at loose ends, now that you have returned."

"Loose ends?" Kepley echoed.

"You do not," Stamford said, choosing his words with care, "seem to me the sort of man to be content merely with making the rounds of social events. And while you do have an estate, the management of it does not seem likely to fully occupy your energy or interests."

"And what do you propose?" Thomas asked, leaning forward, not even aware that he was doing so.

"If you were to find yourself at loose ends," Stamford said, "I might be of assistance in introducing you to someone who is always happy to find another gentleman who is both resourceful and discreet and eager to have something to do."

"I should need some time to consider the matter," Thomas said slowly, "but I think perhaps I might be interested in just such an introduction in, let us say, a couple of month's time? I have, after all, just returned to England, and shall want some time with my wife. But after that . . . Well after that I think that perhaps I would find such an introduction very interesting, indeed."

The two men smiled at each other, in perfect accord.

In another part of town, the scruffy fellow Thomas thought he had seen the day before, moved through the street looking very different. Today he was clean-shaven and dressed as befitted the gentleman he pretended to be.

He was readily admitted at the lodgings of Lord Peter Dalwood. To be sure, the name was unfamiliar to both Dalwood and his valet, but he presented such a sufficiently pleasant demeanor that neither had any hesitation in doing so.

There was a slightly puzzled look in Dalwood's eyes as he greeted his visitor. "Are we acquainted?" he asked when both men were seated with glasses of wine in their hands.

The stranger took a sip of wine before he replied. "Not yet," he said with a thin smile, "but when I have explained, I think you will agree that perhaps we have certain interests in common. Indeed, I believe we might well do each other a good turn."

He paused and Dalwood gestured for the fellow to continue. He was interested, though not greatly so. The stranger's next few words changed all of that.

"I believe we may have a common interest, sir, in confounding Lord Thomas Kepley."

Now Dalwood was fully alert. He was also wary. "What reason have you for thinking I would wish such a thing?" he asked.

The stranger smiled even more. "Your sister. I understand you have reason to believe that Lord Thomas treated her with, er, some unkindness?"

A grim look came into Dalwood's eyes. "Even supposing that were true," he said roughly, "what is your interest in Kepley? And precisely what do you mean when you say we could be of help to each other?"

The stranger explained.

Chapter 13

Lisbeth held up the hem of her riding habit, trying very hard not to show her trepidation. Thomas certainly did not seem to notice.

"Isn't she a beauty?" he asked, holding out a hand to draw her closer to the mare standing saddled at the curb. "And perfectly matched to my gelding."

"A perfect match," Lisbeth agreed.

She swallowed hard and took a few steps closer to the mare. She even managed to make herself reach out to pet the creature's nose. But the moment the gelding turned his head to look at her, she could not help but take a step back. Thomas took it to mean that she was ready to ride.

"I'll throw you up into the saddle," he said, as though it were the easiest thing in the world.

"Of course," she said faintly.

If it was not precisely easy mounting the mare, nonetheless the matter was accomplished all too quickly for Lisbeth's peace of mind. As though she sensed the nervousness of her new mistress, the mare danced sideways and Lisbeth had to tug on the reins to quiet her down.

Fortunately, everyone took it for mere liveliness on the part of the mare, and a very good thing. An attitude that was incomprehensible to Lisbeth.

"I would not want you to think her too tame," Thomas said cheerfully as the mare stepped sideways again.

"Oh, no, never that," Lisbeth replied.

"Good. Well, shall we be off? We cannot gallop here in the city, but I don't doubt that we can find a place along the riding paths to at least canter for a bit. That will be enough excitement for the horses, their first time out, don't you think?"

"Quite enough," Lisbeth agreed.

Indeed, she devoutly hoped they saw no more excitement than a sedate walk. Why, oh, why had she not told Thomas about her fear of horses? It was too late, now that he had purchased this mare for her use. She could not be so ungrateful as to tell him how much she feared the creature. Particularly since her own sense of fairness made her admit that the mare had given her no cause to feel such fear. It was entirely irrational and Lisbeth could not cause the poor mare to suffer for her own nonsense.

Unfortunately, Lisbeth's wish was not granted. It was early enough in the day that very few people were out and about. To be sure, the bridle paths were not entirely deserted, but they were thin enough of company that one could risk a short burst of speed.

Thomas turned to her, a mischievous look in his eyes. "Shall we risk shocking the *ton?*" he said.

"W-what do you mean?"

"A race. With a kiss as the forfeit."

She stared at him, terrified and yet drawn to the boyish look on his face, a look she had not seen since before they were married. How could she disappoint him?

Apparently he took her silence for assent, for the next thing she knew they were racing, side by side, down the bridle path. Lisbeth had done nothing to set her horse in motion, but the mare seemed determined to follow the gelding's lead. With a sense of despair, Lisbeth tried desperately to hold on to her seat—and her breakfast.

Rescue came in the form of a group of Thomas's friends. They cut him off with their own horses, laughing at his good-natured curses.

"I'd heard Kepley had married," one of them told Lisbeth gallantly, "but I had no idea he'd married such a beauty!"

"Tricked you, did he?" another gentleman teased her, sotto voce.

"If you ever tire of him, call upon me and I shall promise to see that you are treated as you deserve," a third gentleman added, with a cheeky grin.

Thomas eased his horse back until he was side by side with Lisbeth. He slipped an arm around her waist and drawled, "You are, all of you, jealous. Simply jealous. I don't blame you, of course. I've married an Incomparable, after all. But she is my wife and I am even more jealous, so not a one of you is to go near her. Is that clear?"

A smile belied his words and for several more moments the young men indulged in that time-honored, but inexplicable to Lisbeth, ritual of bonding by roasting one another ruthlessly. Then, with shouts of laughter, the two parties separated and Thomas and Lisbeth walked their horses side by side again in the now crowded park.

Thomas did his best to keep her attention focused on him. "Do not let the august members of the *ton* see you noticing them," he said in a low voice. "We wish the world to think we are completely wrapped up in each other, as though we cannot bear to be parted, and do not even realize that the rest of the world exists."

Lisbeth was quite happy to follow his lead. She had no wish to be drawn into conversation with anyone, not when she knew how avidly they would be looking for proof or disproof of the rumors they had heard.

And Thomas, when he set himself to the purpose, could be a charming companion. In a surprisingly short time she found herself falling into the old pattern of their friendly banter, before he had asked her to marry him, before he had gone away. It was as if they were simply friends again, though the touch of his hand on her wrist was enough to rouse feelings that reminded Lisbeth he was far more to her than that now.

Thomas was at least as aware of the onlookers as Lisbeth was. He saw the speculative glances, the hastily whispered comments between other riders as they passed. He saw the surprise and confusion on their faces, and he felt more than a little satisfaction at the success of his campaign.

Neither he nor Lisbeth noticed, however, the gentleman with the air of distinction, who watched from a distance. Even if he had seen him, it is unlikely that Thomas would have recognized him as the fellow he had seen on the streets two days before. Nor did he look as he had when Thomas had last encountered him in France. But both Lisbeth and Thomas would have recognized the gentleman with him—Lord Peter Dalwood.

Both men, however, kept to the shadows. Had Thomas seen them, had he recognized the first man, Jean Merlion, for who he was, he would have felt more than alarm. He would have made plans. He certainly would not have simply ridden back to the town house with Lisbeth, feeling as if matters were proceeding quite satisfactorily indeed.

Some hours later, each with a glass of fine brandy in his hand, Sir Robert and Lord Rivendale looked at each other and instantly recognized the expression that meant their wives had rung a peal over their heads.

"Well, how were we to know their sister needed them?" Rivendale protested. "All Lady Thomas's letters claimed she was fine! And that's what she said when she came to visit, too."

"Were we supposed to go spy on her?" Stamford asked. "I can well imagine what our wives would have said if we had tried that!"

"Or were we supposed to somehow know that Kepley was still alive?" Rivendale persisted.

"Probably! And rescued him ourselves into the bargain," Stamford added bitterly.

"Now they expect us to quash all the rumors."

"As if anyone but Kepley and his wife themselves could do that."

"Well, we'd better try. I don't much fancy having Tessa so upset," Rivendale said gloomily.

"No, nor I Alex," Stamford agreed.

"So how do we help them?" Rivendale asked. "Our friends will assume we are merely showing support for the sister of our wives. They are scarcely going to put any credence in what we say!"

For a very long moment, Stamford was silent. Then he smiled. It was a most disconcerting smile. A fanciful person might have called it fiendish.

"I think," he said slowly, "we pretend we do not support Lord and Lady Thomas. I think we pretend to annoyance and impatience and complaint."

"What the devil?" Rivendale demanded. "Do you want our wives to throw us out of our homes?"

Stamford grinned unrepentantly. "No fear of that. They will be perfectly happy with us—once we explain what we are about."

"If you don't explain to me," Rivendale growled, "I daresay I shall plant you a facer! I can make neither heads nor tails of anything you are saying."

Stamford leaned forward. "It is very simple," he said. "You are quite right that anything we say to their favor will be discounted. But complaints will, for that very reason, be believed. So I suggest that we complain that Kepley and his wife go about smelling of April and May and that it is positively indecent how they dote upon each other, for it makes our wives impatient with us! And we shall say that the way Kepley dotes upon his son is causing our wives to insist we do the same with our children

and that we are in dire need of escape before we find ourselves changing nappies!"

Rivendale, who had started to crow with laughter,
suddenly stopped. "Yes, but does Kepley dote upon his
son?" he asked uneasily. "From what Tessa told me, I had
the notion he did not."

Stamford shrugged. "I doubt it matters. It is what he
wishes the *ton* to believe and what our wives wish us to
spread about. Now mind—we shall not volunteer a word
of this! But when pressed to explain our gloomy faces
and short tempers, we will allow ourselves to be persuaded to confide in our listeners. We will pretend to take
no notice of their response."

Rivendale shifted in his chair uneasily. "You have
plenty of practice at deception. I only hope I may carry
off my part as well as you no doubt will do."

"You will do fine," Stamford assured him. "And if in
doubt, simply tell the person to ask me why you are in
such a foul mood! That ought to do the trick."

Rivendale brightened at the notion. Before he had a
chance to pursue the matter, however, he caught sight of
someone in the doorway of the room. Softly he said, "Kepley is here right now. Do we speak to him?"

Stamford rose to his feet in one smooth motion. "Of
course we do, Rivendale," he said calmly. "Of course we
do. Hallo, Kepley! Come join us?"

He did so, albeit a trifle warily. "You both look as if
you are hatching mischief," Thomas said, taking a seat
next to theirs.

"We *are* hatching mischief," Rivendale confirmed,
pitching his voice low enough so that they would not be
overheard.

"And it deals with you," Stamford agreed affably. He
outlined their plan, then said, "Have you any suggestions
to make?"

Thomas hesitated. "Why not say that you have tried to

talk some sense into me and I refuse to listen? That you consider me a traitor to every married gentleman."

That made them laugh, and soon talk turned to other matters. The three men drew interested glances, in part because they were all handsome fellows, and in part because all of London knew their wives were sisters and that Lord Thomas Kepley was newly returned to England.

Still, the most extreme curiosity must eventually give way to boredom or other interests and eventually the three found themselves ignored. It was then that Rivendale said softly, "I have heard about your, er, adventure, Kepley. Congratulations on your safe return."

Thomas frowned. "You may call it an adventure, if you wish," he said curtly. "I had other, far more choice words for the experience, I assure you."

"But you did make it back and the information you brought was invaluable," Stamford said softly. "I understand there are some very important men who speak your name with great gratitude."

"If you are going to speak fustian," Thomas said irritably, "I shall leave!"

"Pray do not do so on my account," Stamford countered, lifting a hand to stop Kepley. "I shall not plague you any more, nor even speak of the matter, if you do not wish me to. I simply thought it as well to let you know that what you did has not gone unappreciated."

Thomas sat back down. "Perhaps not," he said heavily, "but it might well have cost me my chance at happiness. And it most certainly caused my wife a great deal of hardship. Hardship that I am not soon likely to forgive myself for causing her to endure."

It was Rivendale's turn to intervene. He smiled a singularly sweet smile. "Our wives," he told Kepley, "are remarkably resilient women. I've no doubt your wife will soon forgive you and tell you that it doesn't matter—particularly given how important the work was that you were doing."

Kepley stared at him, then at Stamford. "Is there anyone who doesn't know?" he demanded irritably.

"Peace. It is fortunate that Rivendale does know why you were gone so long and why you could not let anyone know you were still alive," Sir Robert replied. "I think you need his help as much as mine in retrieving your wife's reputation. But no one else knows, not even our wives. Though how long that will last before your wife tells them . . ."

"Elizabeth doesn't know," Thomas snapped, "and I will thank you to keep it that way!"

Stamford and Rivendale looked at each other, amusement in their eyes. "She doesn't know. . . ." Rivendale repeated the words slowly.

Stamford shook his head. "That's a mistake."

"Perhaps, but it is mine to make," Thomas retorted. "I will not have her worried over the risks I took. No, nor wondering how soon I may have to go back. It is my job to protect her and that I mean to do, even from knowledge such as this."

"Oh, to be sure, he means to protect her," Rivendale said to Stamford.

"Doesn't know these Barlow women very well, does he?" the other man replied.

"Should like to be there when she finds out," Rivendale continued.

"She won't find out—not if you don't tell her!" Thomas exploded.

"She won't find out?" Stamford looked at him almost with pity. Then, he turned to Rivendale and said, "He thinks she won't find out!" To Thomas he said, "My dear Kepley, haven't you learned yet that wives have a better intelligence system than the ministry?"

"He'll learn," Rivendale prophesized, "and we shall be there when he does."

Kepley cursed them both roundly and then all three men set off to play cards and drink toasts to one another's health.

Very few people noticed Monsieur Jean Merlion sitting in the shadows of the tavern. If they did stare too long, he stared straight back and there was that in his eyes that caused no one to wish to linger. He did not sit alone for long, however. Soon enough two large men joined him. They bent their heads close together and when they eventually rose from the table, it was with the exchange of a small pouch of coins and a clear promise of more.

This was not a tavern that encouraged curiosity and anyone tempted to eavesdrop on the conversations of others had long since been chased away. Still, there was something about these three that drew the eye, even if that same something caused those who looked to shiver and swiftly turn away.

And no one even tried to follow either party out the door. Not when the hilt of a workmanlike dagger was displayed so openly. Not when the first of the three had a look in his eye that made one think he might like dispatching people to their Maker.

No, the three men departed from the tavern in peace. Indeed, more than one sigh of relief greeted the same. And soon the darkness swallowed up the three men and their plans.

A little over an hour later, Monsieur Merlion entered another, far more elegantly furnished room than the one he had so recently left. The company was also more select, for he had entered the portals of one of London's more exclusive gaming clubs. Because Lord Peter Dalwood had brought the Frenchman, there were few who refused to accept him, declaring by the end of the evening that he was an amiable fellow.

A hint of an accent colored his speech and would have

endeared him to the ladies, had there been any present tonight. But this was a gentleman's preserve and so he had to settle for merely being considered acceptable.

He studied the room with a languid gaze and apparent indifference to most of the company—including the man he had particularly come to see. Lord Thomas Kepley looked very different than when last they had met, but so too did he. For the briefest of moments a grim expression crossed his face, so much so that more than one person looked twice to see if they had mistaken the matter. Someone asked if he were feeling ill. He waved away the suggestion with a laugh and turned his whole attention to the current game of cards—or so it seemed, at any rate, to anyone who might have been paying attention.

In truth, he missed nothing of what Lord Thomas or his companions did. He tossed out casual questions about many of the gentlemen present tonight and in the end gained the information he had been seeking about Kepley. Once he had that, he lingered awhile so as not to be conspicuous in his pursuit, but he left as soon as he judged it safe to do so. He had too much to do to waste the night in foolish games.

Dalwood stayed behind. No doubt he hoped not to be tied too closely to the Frenchman later. Merlion smiled mirthlessly at the thought. Lord Peter would inevitably be tied to Lady Thomas's disappearance. But let him hope to be able to avoid the finger of blame, if he chose. He would discover the truth soon enough.

Chapter 14

Lisbeth held Tom on her lap. He was smiling today, and she could not help being grateful that thus far his good health had held. Beside her in the carriage, Aunt Margaret pursed her lips in obvious disapproval of the way the coachman handled the reins. Nor was she pleased when Kepley roasted her by saying that when they returned to the country she might drive the coach herself, if she was so dissatisfied with the coachman.

"I don't wish to drive a carriage like this one. I wish the coachman to do his job properly!" Miss Winsham retorted roundly.

But in truth, Margaret had no real reason for the megrims that now assailed her. As much as she had needed to worry about her niece these past twenty months, Elizabeth and Lord Thomas now seemed in a fair way to being reconciled. And the child seemed to be thriving as well. So why was she blue-deviled in this foolish way?

Was it the fear that she was no longer needed? No, for Margaret had long chafed at being tied to Elizabeth's side and thus unable to continue doing what had always been so important to her—rescuing children. And while Tom might be healthy for the moment, there would always be a need for the herbal teas Margaret could brew for him. No, it was nothing so simple as that.

An image, of a somewhat older gentleman, a rough-tongued fellow of science and medicine, rose in Margaret's mind. She ruthlessly suppressed it. She would not think of Dr. Brooks! He despised her, or at any rate felt her to be an unwomanly sort of creature, even if he did respect her use of herbs. He had made it clear that he felt women ought not to trouble their heads over such things, and how could she possibly find herself drawn to a man with such impossible views as that?

But she was, and it was a most lowering reflection. Had her wits gone wanting? Surely, at her age, she was past the danger of foolish infatuation! Why, then, did she find herself thinking of the man, wishing she could hear his voice, and wanting to see his face? They would only be at odds if he were to appear.

Still, she mustn't inflict her irritation upon Kepley or Elizabeth. Neither of them deserved her Friday face. Indeed, it was her duty to be a support to both of them—at least for the moment.

Lord Thomas's coachman neatly turned the barouche into the park and drove to a spot of green grass where they might let Tom toddle about a bit. Kepley and Elizabeth would no doubt, at some point, wander off to be alone, and Margaret would watch out for the child. The nursery maid was scandalized that she was not to accompany them, but her protests had been overruled by, as it seemed, the fond parents.

In truth, it was not entirely a lie. Kepley, for all his protests that he did not believe Tom was his son, nonetheless was unmistakably growing fond of the boy. And that pleased Margaret. She wished he would accept the truth, but if he could not, at least he did not mean to hold the child to account for what he believed to be the sins of the mother.

Margaret was deep in just such thoughts when a familiar voice called out to their party. "Hallo, Lord Thomas! And Lady Thomas! And Miss Winsham. How is the lad doing, here in London?"

They turned to greet Dr. Brooks, who hurried to catch

up with them. Margaret waited as the pleasantries were exchanged. Her breath seemed to catch in her throat and for once she could think of nothing to say.

It was impossible! And yet, there he was—Dr. Brooks. How was she to greet him? How was she to behave?

Margaret stiffened as she watched Elizabeth and Kepley welcome the man with great good humor. As if they were glad to see him! She merely sniffed and tilted her nose into the air. She would not give him the satisfaction of seeing that she, too, was pleased to see him again.

But then he turned and looked at her, really looked at her. There was both pleasure and trepidation in his eyes, just as there was in hers. And while there was condescension in his voice, he spoke in such a way that she could not help but know that he was roasting her.

"Miss Winsham! It is a delight to see you as well. I suppose you are setting London on its ears with your unorthodox treatments? Meddling and turning established wisdom upside down?"

Margaret meant to snub him, for that would be far safer for her, far safer for him—or so she told herself. But she could not do it. Not when he looked at her in such a way! Not when he held out his hand to her in such a friendly fashion.

"What are you doing here in London?" Margaret asked as she took it, reveling in the feel of her hand in his. "I—we thought you were fixed in the country."

He smiled and said, still holding on to her hand, "I have written a paper and mean to present it to the Society tonight. It is on the subject of useful herbs in cases of difficulty in breathing. I hope you will wish me luck."

Now Margaret did pull free her hand. There was no longer a welcome in her eyes or softness in her voice as she replied, "I see. You have wasted no time in claiming credit."

His eyes seemed to dance in a most unseemly way, and

his good humor was not in the least overset by the way she snapped at him.

"My dear lady," Dr. Brooks replied, "I did not claim credit in my paper. Indeed, I make it quite clear that I am merely reporting my observations on the work of a very talented herbalist whom I refer to as M. Winsham."

She ought not to care, not really. Certainly she ought not to feel such an absurd degree of pleasure at his words. But Margaret did. Indeed, she blushed a most charming shade of pink—or so Kepley told her teasingly.

"I think the two of you ought to take a walk so that Dr. Brooks can tell you all about it, Aunt Margaret. Thomas and I shall take care of Tom," Elizabeth added with a smile.

She ought to have protested, she really should have, but instead Margaret found herself being shepherded down a path with the doctor at her side. Since she had no choice, she decided, she might as well enjoy herself.

Lord Peter watched the two older people walk away from Lord Thomas and his wife and child. With Miss Winsham gone, it was one less person to take into account. Still, if he was to do as Monsieur Merlion wished him to do, he needed to separate Kepley from his wife and child as well before the plan could go into effect. Particularly as the family picture, as it was, drew too many fascinated eyes. Few would have paid attention to Lord Thomas's wife and child if they were by themselves. But Kepley's presence drew a great deal of interest and speculation.

Dalwood might have been tempted to try anyway, but Monsieur Merlion was there and he was not a man given to foolishness. He knew when to step back and revise his plans before he tried to act. This was unmistakably one of those times.

Quietly, so quietly that no one noticed, he touched

Dalwood on the arm and they both slipped away, back to where the other men were waiting, and gave them new orders, orders they were perfectly willing to follow.

"What is it, Thomas?" Lisbeth asked, concerned at the look on Kepley's face.

Startled, he turned toward her. "What do you mean?" he asked lightly.

"You looked upset. As though you had seen someone you greatly dislike," Lisbeth said. "Who is it?"

For a moment, she thought he would tell her. Then he seemed to change his mind. He shrugged and said, "It is of no importance. I am certain I am mistaken anyway. Tell me, what do you think of Dr. Brooks's sudden appearance in London? And Miss Winsham's reaction to it?"

Lisbeth wanted to shake him, to demand that Thomas confide in her. There were, she thought, far too many secrets between them. But, in the end, her courage failed her and she answered with a lightness to match his own. "I think that perhaps we shall be seeing a great deal of the doctor while he is in London."

Some of the tension seemed to go out of his shoulders, and Thomas chuckled. "I should think you are right. Ought we to invite Dr. Brooks to dinner?"

Lisbeth shook her head. "Aunt Margaret would never forgive us for interfering in such a way. I shouldn't like to face her wrath, would you?"

Thomas pretended to shudder. "Indeed not!" He gave a mock sigh. "I suppose Dr. Brooks must simply find his own way to court your aunt, if that is what he wishes. Ah, keep smiling. We have drawn a certain degree of notice and I think someone is coming to speak to us. Give me Tom to hold and pretend to take no notice of anyone until they speak to us directly."

"Lord Thomas! Lady Thomas! How intriguing to find you in the park with a baby. It is your child, I presume?"

The carriage had pulled to a halt at the edge of the grass. Seated in it were three ladies who were avidly staring at Lisbeth, Tom, and Kepley. It was evident they thought it an astonishing sight. Thomas was the one who answered them. He chuckled and smiled down at Tom, then looked at the ladies.

"Ladies, may I present to you my son? He is a trifle young, of course, to be hanging out for a bride, but in twenty-five years or so, perhaps you could keep him in mind for one of your daughters or granddaughters?"

Lisbeth smiled sweetly, not daring to trust herself to speak. In any event, it was far more amusing to watch the three ladies struggle for something to reply. It was evident that they had not expected Thomas to openly acknowledge the child as his own and he had neatly spiked the set downs they had been prepared to give.

The ladies murmured something suitable and then signaled for their driver to go on. Kepley held on to his son until they were out of sight. Then he passed the child to Lisbeth, but only long enough for her to put him down on the grass. Already there were other carriages driving over to where they stood and Thomas once again scooped up the child and repeated the same performance as before.

And it was a performance. For all his smiles and kind words, there was a strain about his eyes. For all he pretended to dote on Tom, there were moments in between when a bleakness crossed his face and Lisbeth knew he still could not bring himself to believe the boy was his son.

Lisbeth alternated between warmth at his kindness in doing what he could to deny the rumors, and anger that he could not trust his heart over his head. For if he had, he must have known, looking into eyes that were so like his own, that Tom truly was his son.

Still, she knew she was very fortunate. Another man

would not have been so kind, another man would not
have done so much to try to protect a child he did not
think was his own. Another man would not have done
what he could to smooth the path for Dr. Brooks's pursuit
of Aunt Margaret when the pair returned from their prom-
enade.

"Will you come to the house to examine the child?"
Thomas asked, as though it were a matter of great urgency.

The physician frowned. "Should I examine him here,
now, if you are worried?"

"No, no," Thomas replied hastily. "Tomorrow afternoon would be soon enough. It is nothing urgent. I simply thought I should like to hear your opinion of whether
the London air has been unhealthy for him or not."

Dr. Brooks snorted. "I can tell you that without any
more ado! The London air is unhealthy for everyone!
Still, I suppose a short visit may or may not have hurt the
poor lad. I suppose I could come examine the child. But
as I am already here . . ."

"Oh, but it would attract a great deal of attention if you
examined him now," Lisbeth improvised. "Why, he
might start to scream, and you can well imagine how dis-
tasteful such a display would be to all of us. Please say
you will come around tomorrow afternoon!"

He took several moments to answer. The physician
looked from Lisbeth to Thomas and back again. He
seemed fascinated by the locket at her throat, and she had
to stop herself from covering it with her hand. Indeed, he
took so long to answer, that Lisbeth began to think he
meant to refuse. But in the end, he didn't.

"That is a fascinating locket," he murmured. "It reminds me of something, but I cannot think quite what."

Abruptly he seemed to shake his head to clear it, and
then Dr. Brooks looked Lisbeth straight in the eyes. There
was a quirk of the eyebrows and a glint of amusement in
his expression.

"I cannot come tomorrow afternoon. I am otherwise occupied. Perhaps the next day would do just as well?"

"Er, yes, of course," Lisbeth replied.

"I rather thought it might," the physician murmured.

Lisbeth did not quite know how to answer that, but Thomas said all that was proper. Then Dr. Brooks again turned to Aunt Margaret. His smile seemed somehow warmer as he bowed to her and said, "I look forward to seeing you the day after tomorrow, Miss Winsham. I shall, of course, wish to consult with you on the boy's condition."

Aunt Margaret blushed again. Lisbeth could not help but stare because, before the advent of the physician, she could not recollect ever seeing her aunt caught off guard in such a way. It was most disconcerting, and more than a little enchanting. Still, Lisbeth forbore to tease her aunt. Instead, she set about gathering up their things. It was time to return home with Tom. He was growing tired, and soon his fascination with grass and carriages and so many new faces would turn to something far less pleasing.

Chapter 15

Thomas saw Elizabeth just as she was about to go out the front door. "Where are you going?" he asked.

She stopped and turned to look at him, clearly taken aback by his tone. "I am going to Hatchard's," she replied, not trying to hide her astonishment at his manner.

"I shall go with you," Thomas said, not even knowing himself why he felt such urgency.

"That isn't necessary."

"Nonetheless, I wish to do so."

Elizabeth stared at Thomas. So did the footman who had been about to open the door for her. Thomas felt his neck cloth seem to tighten about his throat.

"And if I should prefer to go alone?" she asked, her voice a challenge.

Thomas knew that his expression as well as his voice was cold and forbidding, but he could not help himself. "You will wait for me," he said.

Abruptly, Elizabeth ceased to argue. Thomas was not fooled into thinking she had yielded completely. Still, she waited and allowed him to hand her into the carriage and take his place at her side.

Once they were on their way, however, Elizabeth said, in a voice that betrayed her anger, "I am accustomed, Thomas, to going out and about on my own. I did so for the twenty months you were gone."

It was a perfectly reasonable argument. And had it not been for the thought that, unlikely as it seemed, Jean

Merlion might be in London, Thomas would have agreed. Instead, he replied, "Nevertheless, you will not do so while we are here in London."

"Why not?" she demanded.

He understood her bewilderment, but how to answer? He could not tell her about Merlion. Not without telling her things he did not know if he could ever bring himself to say. But he had to keep her safe and so he took refuge in a partial truth.

"I have told you," Thomas said in a voice that he hoped was sufficiently aloof to daunt her, "it is important to show the *ton* that we are a devoted couple."

"Surely we have done so already," Elizabeth persisted. "And in any event, it cannot possibly matter whether or not there are some occasions on which I go here or there on my own. After all, you do so all the time."

Thomas felt more than a hint of desperation. "That is different," he said.

"How so?"

Again Thomas took refuge in a partial truth. "I am your husband. Of course I go off on my own, from time to time. It is to be expected."

"I understand that," Elizabeth said with exaggerated patience. "Nor do I object. I simply do not see why I cannot do the same."

Thomas had to fight the urge to mop his brow. "Isn't it enough that I do not wish you to do so?" he demanded.

"No."

"But I am your husband," he repeated.

"You keep saying those words," Elizabeth retorted, with what even Thomas considered pardonable exasperation, "but I do not see what difference that makes! Many wives go out and about alone. And while I would not choose to do something that would completely overset your wishes, I cannot see that going to Hatchard's on my own is of any great importance."

"Why must you question everything I say?" Thomas grumbled.

"Why should I not?" she countered. "I have been accustomed to managing, with only Aunt Margaret to help, for some twenty months. Why should I behave as though I were wanting in wits simply because you have come home? I cannot and I will not do so! If you want me to do as you wish, you will have to tell me why. If the reasons make sense, then no doubt I will do as you ask. But it is outside of enough to expect me to hand over my independence of mind and spirit simply because we have exchanged wedding vows!"

Thomas flinched. He could neither deny the justice of her words nor tell her the truth, because that would mean telling her about Merlion. What the devil was he to say? That a Frenchman with a wish for revenge might be in London? It was absurd! And yet, his instincts told him that it was indeed possible. And it was just those instincts that had kept Thomas alive while he was in France.

But because it was so unlikely that Merlion was really here, and because he did not wish to alarm Elizabeth unless he was certain, Thomas was at a loss for what to say to her. Fortunately, the carriage had drawn to a halt and he was spared the necessity of answering.

Elizabeth was not in the best of moods as they entered Hatchard's lending library. Her temper frayed even further when Thomas hovered about as she chose her books. He knew that he was being foolish, because even if Merlion was in London, he would not dare to attack either of them here. But Thomas could not help himself.

"I do not see," he said shortly, "why you must come here for books when my parents already have such an extensive library."

"They do not have the books I wish to read," Elizabeth retorted.

"Rubbish," Thomas said dismissively.

"Indeed?" she asked, a dangerous glint in her eyes.

"That is only your opinion, of course. And, in any event, it is my rubbish, my choice."

"Yes, but it means a pointless expedition to this place."

"I did not ask you to come. Indeed," Elizabeth said, clearly fighting a losing battle to hold on to her temper, "I asked you not to come! You might have stayed home and never been troubled by what books I wished to read or where I went to get them. You need never have known I was doing something of which you so patently disapprove."

"You are being absurd!"

"Perhaps, but no more so than you, sir."

That was quite sufficient to have them not speaking to each other—a state that lasted the entire way home. The footman who opened the door to them was the same one who had watched them leave the house earlier and he seemed to take great interest in the expressions on their faces.

"Have our horses brought around," Thomas told him curtly. "My wife and I are going out riding."

Elizabeth stared up at him. "I am not," she said.

"Of course you are. We agreed that we would be seen together in the park every day," Thomas told her impatiently. "Go change into your habit. By the time we are ready, no doubt our horses will be here."

Elizabeth wanted to object; he could see it in her face. But in the end she turned and headed up the stairs. Thomas slowly followed.

Miss Winsham had no notion of the contretemps between Elizabeth and Kepley. She left the house without hearing anything of their discourse. Nor would she have paid it any attention if she had, so caught up was she in her own concerns. She was thinking of Dr. Brooks.

It was foolish beyond permission, of course, to think that he could have an interest in her. Once she had believed in love. She had also believed in the locket. Time had taught her wisdom and cynicism so that now she believed only in the doctor's interest in her remedies.

No, it would be better to focus her attention where it was needed, than to waste her time on nonsense such as romantic emotions. Her London friends were expecting her, this morning, to check on Hope, and to see to the health of some of the children they were housing until new homes could be found for them. To that end, Miss Winsham carried with her some of her tonics and herbs.

She was examining the tongue of a young lad whose throat hurt when she heard a familiar voice behind her saying, "Well, well, well."

For a moment, Margaret thought she must have been imagining things. But she wasn't. When she turned around to look, she found Dr. Brooks standing behind her, watching her with a bemused look upon his face.

They spoke at the same moment, the same words, "What on earth are you doing here?"

They paused and waited, each for the other to speak. At last the doctor gestured for her to answer first. Margaret bristled and said, "I always come here when I am in London. These children are a particular interest of mine. But what are you doing here?"

He smiled, wistfully, it seemed. "They are a particular interest of mine, as well," he said. "And for the past year I have made it a point to regularly check on them. I removed to the country for reasons of health and could not resist, while I was here, coming to see the children again. I suppose it will sound foolish to you, but I have missed them."

Margaret felt her throat go very dry. "It does not sound foolish to me," she managed to reply. "It does not sound foolish at all."

And then he swept past all her carefully erected defenses and shattered all the armor still left around her heart, when he said, "Will you allow me to assist you, Miss Winsham?"

Her voice sounded very strange to her, so oddly unsteady, as Margaret replied, "Yes, Dr. Brooks. I think I should be very glad if you would."

In another part of town, Alex and Tessa were preparing to take a drive around the park. Part of their purpose was the hope of seeing Lisbeth. The unhappiness they had seen in her face and heard in her voice, the day they visited, worried them. And while they might have called upon her again at the Marquess of Aylsham's town house, they had heard about her daily visits to the park with Kepley and wished to see for themselves what the two were about. Perhaps that was why they were so quick to spot her when she and Lord Kepley rode their horses on a nearby bridle path.

"She's on a horse!" Tessa said in astonishment.

"He must have forced her to it," Alex said, a grim line about her mouth.

"Or he asked and she didn't tell him she was afraid," Tessa pointed out.

Alex admitted the possibility reluctantly. "True." She sighed. "I wish that Lisbeth had more resolution."

"She loves Kepley, I think," Tessa answered softly. "And that no doubt makes her sway to his wishes. It was the same for both of us."

"Well," Alex said with great resolution, "in that event, there is only one thing to do—we must tell him for her."

Alex immediately gave directions to the coachman to take them closer to the bridle path. There she did not hesitate to signal to her sister and Kepley. If either felt any reluctance obeying the summons, they did not show it. Instead they came toward the open carriage with every appearance of being pleased to see Lisbeth's sisters.

At least until they were close by. Then Lisbeth let her

horse fall back a little and left it to Thomas to greet her sisters first. Perhaps she sensed they would ask questions she did not wish to answer.

"Good afternoon, Lady Stamford. Lady Rivendale," Thomas said with an easy smile.

Tessa smiled shyly, but Alex was determined to storm the walls before Thomas could possibly retreat. "Do you know that our sister is frightened of horses?" she demanded.

"Frightened?" Thomas looked honestly taken aback.

"Yes, frightened," Alex repeated, ruthlessly pressing her advantage. "And yet you have her mounted on a horse. And you are riding out where any chance thing could cause her horse to startle."

"But she never told me!" Thomas protested. "Did you, Elizabeth?"

He turned to have her confirm his words and discovered that she was gone. From the astonished expressions on the faces of her sisters, he gathered they had not seen her leave either. Swiftly he looked around, trying to spy where she had gone, but without success. Impatience gave way to irritation, which, in turn, gave way to concern. It did not help that Lady Stamford gave him the sharp side of her tongue.

"So now she runs away from you? It does not speak well to the way you have been treating her."

Goaded beyond discretion or manners, Thomas ripped up at Lisbeth's sister. "The devil take it, woman! I have only been trying to protect Elizabeth and keep her safe and show her how to go on!"

"Of course you have," Tessa said cordially. "But did you ever stop to ask what she wished?"

"Of course I did!"

"Ah, but did you listen to what she said?"

Thomas flushed. "You will forgive me, ladies," he said, ignoring the hit, "for I must go find my wife. It shouldn't be hard. The park is too crowded for her to have gone very far."

But Thomas was mistaken. Elizabeth was nowhere to be found. No one seemed to have seen where she had gone; no one seemed to know where she might be. It was impossible to think that no one had noticed anything, but that was how it seemed. He ought to have kept asking, of course, but he didn't. Nor did Tessa and Alex. It was too easy for all three of them to believe that Elizabeth had simply gone home, so as to be off her mare as quickly as possible and to avoid their questions.

Why the devil hadn't she told him how she felt? Thomas demanded silently. Why the devil hadn't she confided in him her fears?

A tiny voice argued that he would not have understood; he would have urged her to overcome her fears. But it was a voice he did not wish to hear and so he shut it out quite ruthlessly, determined to go home and ring a peal over his wife's heedless head.

Lisbeth regarded Lord Peter Dalwood with gratitude—at least at first. He was the perfect gentleman, offering to help her by escorting her home because she suddenly felt ill on her horse. She ought to have told Thomas and her sisters that she was going, but she could not bear to step into the middle of their contretemps. So instead she had been grateful for Dalwood's offer.

And then, suddenly, as they reached the gates of the park a change came over him. His hand seized her bridle, and with a look of triumph on his face, Dalwood forced Lisbeth's mare in a different direction, one that quickly led to dark streets and alleyways and a waiting carriage into which he bundled her without ceremony.

She heard him give swift orders over his shoulder to someone to take her mare and let it loose twenty miles to the north of London. Then he shut the door with Lisbeth inside. But he did not join her.

Since the shades had been drawn and even tied shut, it was dark in the carriage, but she had caught a glimpse of someone just before Dalwood shut the door. As the carriage clattered forward, Lisbeth stared at the stranger. "Who are you?" she demanded.

Slowly her eyes adjusted. The man sitting opposite her took some time before he answered.

"I think it would be as well if you didn't know," he answered, a hint of steel in his voice.

Lisbeth heard the accent in his voice. He was French, of course. There were a great many French émigrés in London these days. But he did not have the air of one. He was too angry, too self-assured. She tried to prod him into further speech, in hopes that he would tell her his plans.

"W-where are you t-taking m-me?" she asked, pretending to stammer.

He smiled a pitying smile. "Again, it is better that you do not know," he replied. "We may hope your stay will be a short one, but I suggest that *madame* resigns herself to a possible long visit in my care."

Madame? For some reason, the way he spoke the word frightened Lisbeth and she shivered.

"Are you cold?" he asked solicitously. "I should not have thought it, on such a warm day. But if you wish, I can perhaps find a rug to wrap around you."

"No, no. That is quite all right," Lisbeth said.

She could feel him smile, even though she could not see him in the dim light that seeped around the edges of the shades. "Good. I suggest you rest, *madame*. We have a long journey before us. I hope you do not mind the water?"

"Water?" Lisbeth echoed warily.

"You do not suffer from seasickness?"

"I cannot say," she answered honestly. "I have never been on a boat."

He laughed softly, and it was a sound that chilled her to the core. "By tonight, *madame,* you will be."

When Thomas reached his parents' London town house, he discovered Elizabeth was not there and that she had not been seen since she had left with him, riding on her mare. A footman dispatched to the stables returned to say her mare had not returned, either. The fellow gave him the oddest look and it occurred to Thomas that soon the tale would be all over the household that Elizabeth had run away from him. That was enough to send him into a quiet parlor to think.

The odds were that she was simply upset with him. But what if it were more than that? Now he wished that he had confided in Stamford and Rivendale the possibility that Jean Merlion had followed him to London. Because if the Frenchman had done so, and that was who she was with, then there was no time to be lost. But if she was not with Merlion, then all he would do was destroy every effort he had made to retrieve his and Elizabeth's reputation if he made public her disappearance.

A moment was more than enough for Thomas to reach his conclusion. Elizabeth's safety outweighed any other consideration. But part of keeping her safe might mean not letting anyone know what he feared. He must, once again, play a part and trust that Stamford and Rivendale would play theirs as promised.

First he went in search of Miss Winsham. To his surprise, he found her in her room, sitting on her bed and just staring at the wall, lost in thought. At the sight of him, she straightened and her voice was as brisk as ever as she asked what he wanted.

"Have you seen Elizabeth?" Thomas asked.

She shook her head. "I was told she had gone out riding with you."

Diverted, Thomas asked, "Is she afraid of horses?"

"Ever since she was thrown by one when she was four," Miss Winsham said tartly.

"How was I to know that?" Thomas demanded angrily. "No one, including Elizabeth or you, saw fit to tell me so!"

"You could have asked why she was reluctant."

Thomas sighed. "Yes, yes. I have failed abominably as a husband. You are not the first today to tell me so. But that is not why I came to find you. I wish to know if you have any notion where Elizabeth might have gone. She disappeared while we were out riding in the park."

Miss Winsham neither cried out in dismay nor tried to tell him that his fears were nonsense. Instead she asked him to put her in possession of the facts. Then, when he was done, she took a moment to consider the matter before she spoke.

"You had better go look for her. Get Stamford and Rivendale to help. If she returns while you are gone, I shall send word to both their houses."

Kepley nodded. "But mind," he said, "I don't wish anyone else to know she is gone. Or, rather, that I don't know where she has gone. Not unless it becomes absolutely necessary."

Miss Winsham's eyes narrowed suspiciously. "Why not?" she demanded.

"I still hope to persuade London that it was a love match between us," Thomas said. "If the rumor gets about that she has run away from me, it will put paid to my efforts."

It didn't take long for him to change yet again. This time he wore the clothes of a gentleman looking for a bit of sport on the town. To the footman, he said carelessly, "I am off to see Lord Stamford and Lord Rivendale. Should my wife return within the hour, pray send to let me know."

"Yes, sir."

And so Thomas swept out of the house and set off

down the street at a languid pace intended to convince anyone watching that he had not a care in the world. He hoped that he had no need for concern. But he very much feared that he did.

At Stamford's house he was promptly admitted to the drawing room, where he found Lady Stamford regaling her husband with what she believed to be a list of Thomas's failings. At the sight of him, her eyes narrowed and she demanded, "Well? Was my sister at home?"

Thomas bowed to her. "That, Lady Stamford, is something I wish to discuss, in private, with your husband."

He ought to have known she would protest. But a few words, softly spoken by her husband, were enough to send her to another room. And then Thomas told Stamford about Elizabeth's disappearance. About Merlion, he only said that a Frenchman might have taken her.

The other man listened, then nodded. "Very well. We shall collect Rivendale and begin our search. We must assume the worst, but, in any event, our first efforts must be at the clubs. Perhaps someone there will have a tale to tell of someone who saw her flee from you. Or noticed if she was taken."

Chapter 16

Jean Merlion glared at Lady Thomas Kepley in frustration. She was supposed to be cowed. She ought to be crying. She should not have had the audacity to bite his thumb! A bruise on her cheek testified to the strength of his anger.

The men he had hired to help were watching with amusement, and that did not help Merlion's mood. Under his feet, the boat rocked alarmingly and he felt it was further proof of her unnatural nature that she seemed to take the motion far more easily than he did.

Indeed, Lady Thomas might have been sitting at home, in her drawing room, for all the lack of composure she revealed. She dared to smile as he cursed her.

"It was a mistake, you know, to take me," she said in a conversational tone. "I don't take well to such things. Papa was a brute, much like you are, and if he could not frighten me then you haven't much chance of doing so either. Threats, you see, only make me angry. And I don't think you are going to like me when I am angry."

"*Madame,*" Merlion said, not even trying to hide his rage, "I already dislike you intensely!"

"Sir, before this adventure is over, I promise you will have good reason to dislike me even more."

That was not what Merlion wished to hear. But then nothing had gone quite as planned thus far, so why should he expect things to change now? He certainly didn't think she was likely to become more amenable, no matter what he did. Particularly since he had the uneasy feeling Lady Thomas was telling the truth when she said that threats would only make her angrier. That would fit with everything she had said and done thus far.

But it didn't matter, Merlion told himself. Where they were going, anger or fear wouldn't help the woman. What mattered was how Lord Thomas was reacting to the disappearance of his wife. Had he found the letter yet, telling him to go and speak with Dalwood? Had that gentleman told him yet where his wife was to be found? Had he decided whether or not to follow?

He could not imagine any man not following to reclaim his wife—even if he despised her, as rumor first suggested Kepley might. But Lord Thomas did not despise his wife. That much had been evident from his behavior over the past week or so. Which meant that he had all the more reason to follow. And when he did . . . Ah, then it would be time for revenge.

Thomas looked around. No one was paying them any great attention, but nonetheless he took Stamford's arm, and Rivendale's, as if they were just three friends out for an evening of fun, and pushed them toward the door of the club.

"Let us go somewhere more private to talk," he suggested in a low voice that could not possibly be overheard.

Outside the three men climbed into the closed carriage and held their conference while the coachman drove the streets at random.

"No one seems to have seen anything, except at the park. No one saw her after she left or even seems to know she is missing," Stamford reported.

"Dalwood appears to have been the last one to speak with her," Rivendale added, "but no one seems to know what she might have said to him and he was not there to ask."

Thomas grew more and more alarmed with every apparently innocuous bit of information he heard. "Let us go round to Lord Peter's lodgings and speak with him there," he said grimly.

"Perhaps we should check back at your father's town house and see if she has returned first," Stamford suggested.

Reluctantly, Thomas nodded and then rapped on the roof of the carriage, causing the coachman to pull to a halt. The new direction was quickly given and a short time later they arrived at the Marquess of Aylsham's house.

Rivendale and Stamford waited in the carriage while Thomas ran up the steps. But he did not even go in the door, for the butler who greeted Kepley also handed him a letter. Thomas read the missive twice. It made no sense to him, but he thanked the fellow and then turned and rejoined the two men in the carriage—after he gave the coachman orders to take them to Dalwood's lodgings.

"Well?" Rivendale asked.

Thomas looked at him. "There is a note, and ironically it tells me to go and speak with Lord Peter, if I wish to know where Elizabeth is."

"Dalwood? What the devil has he to do with any of this?" Stamford asked.

"He was the last one seen speaking with her," Thomas reminded Sir Robert.

"Yes, but Dalwood was also seen speaking to several people shortly after he was seen speaking with your wife," Rivendale objected. "He couldn't possibly have had time to take her anywhere."

"Perhaps not, but he may very well know something about this anyway," Thomas countered.

Stamford, however, had been watching Thomas's face. "What else was there about the letter to worry you?" he asked.

"It was signed by a man I have good reason to fear," Thomas answered grimly.

"Tell us about him," Stamford said. "Is it the Frenchman?"

Thomas hesitated. He looked at both of them. "This is entirely in confidence, you understand?" The other men nodded, and Thomas went on. "As you know, I was not a prisoner of war the entire time. I managed to slip behind enemy lines and find out some very important information. While I was doing so, I encountered a Frenchman who took a particular interest in my activities. We disliked each other, even beyond the fact that our two countries were at war."

"And you think he is the one who has Elizabeth?" Stamford said slowly.

"But would he dare come into this country?" Rivendale asked. "And how would he do so? Might not someone recognize him?"

Thomas grimaced. "We are, in theory, at peace with France, and this man is adept at disguises. I thought perhaps I had seen him on the street, but told myself I must be mistaken. It would be just like him to enlist the aid of Lord Peter and just like Dalwood to agree."

"What would he do with her, this Frenchman?" Rivendale asked quietly.

Thomas turned to stare at him. "Use her for revenge. He will want to hurt me, as he believes I hurt him. If this letter says to go see Dalwood, it is because Dalwood can tell me where the Frenchman took her. Because he will want me to follow."

The carriage drew to a halt outside Dalwood's lodgings. "Shall we come in with you?" Rivendale asked.

Thomas hesitated and Stamford said, "The sight of all three of us might persuade him to tell you what he knows more quickly."

"So it might," Thomas agreed. "Come along then, and let us see what Dalwood has to say."

Lord Peter had not been expecting company. Indeed, he seemed about to go out for the evening and tried to say so when the three men were shown in to his chambers.

"Later," Thomas said. "For now, I wish to ask you about my wife."

Dalwood blinked. He looked away and pretended a great interest in a point upon the wall. "Lady Thomas? I last saw her in the park. She said she was feeling faint and meant to go home. Isn't she there?"

Stamford stepped toward the man. "Kepley has received a letter that seems to indicate you know something more than that."

"A l-l-letter?" Dalwood stammered.

"From Monsieur Merlion," Thomas confirmed.

Dalwood frowned. "I don't know any Frenchman named Merlion."

"Perhaps he used another name?" Rivendale suggested.

"You do know a Frenchman," Stamford said, and it was not a question, for he had been watching the other man closely.

"I know a great many French émigrés," Dalwood agreed. "What is that to say to anything? Everyone does!"

"This particular Frenchman," Thomas said softly as he advanced on Dalwood, "would have had a special interest in my wife. And he sent me this letter saying that if I wished to know where she was, I should come see you. Now, I suggest you tell me what you know without any further lies. I am growing impatient."

"We all are growing impatient," Stamford chimed in.

"Very impatient," Rivendale agreed.

Dalwood was essentially a coward. He took several steps backward and tripped over a chair. His back against the wall, he became defiant. "Whatever his name is, he said he was taking her to France. Said you wouldn't have the courage to follow, but he hoped you did. Said he would do to you what you did to him."

Thomas stood very still. It was Stamford who asked, "Where? When?"

Dalwood named a small seaport town. "He means to sail on the next tide. You cannot possibly catch up with him. You will have to go all the way to France. And there the advantage will lie with him!"

"I shall catch him," Thomas said with quiet certainty.

"Will you?" Dalwood asked softly. "Perhaps. Though I cannot think why you should wish to do so. She isn't worthy to be your wife, you know. She never was. Not like my sister. Anna would have made you a very suitable wife. And if you hadn't betrayed her, she would still be alive. But go after your wife, if you choose. Perhaps he will kill you. Perhaps you will succeed in rescuing her. Did you know, by the by, that while you were gone she was taking in sewing? Yes, earning money with her needle—and who knows how else?"

Without a word, Thomas stepped forward and planted Dalwood a facer. The fellow crumpled to the floor, but Thomas didn't wait to see how he was. Instead he turned and left the room. His friends followed.

Down on the street, Thomas paused. For a long moment, they were all silent. None of them quite knew what to say about Dalwood's words. Finally it was Rivendale who cleared his throat, and said, "I do not think there is any time to waste. What do you mean to do, Kepley?"

There was no expression on Thomas's face, no hint of emotion in his voice, as he replied, "Go after them. All the way to France, if need be."

"How?"

"It might," Thomas said, with a wry twist to his mouth, "be better if you didn't know."

"But we will," Stamford replied softly. "Because we are going with you."

Before Thomas could object, Rivendale placed a hand on his arm. "We go with you," he echoed Stamford.

"For all the *ton* might think us foppish dandies," Stamford persisted, "Rivendale and I do have some experience in such things. You ought to know that, for you were with us when we went down to the docks to try to rescue Lady Rivendale and Miss Winsham."

He ought to object, Thomas thought. But he could read the determination in their faces and he understood the justice in Stamford's words. And with their help he would have a much better chance of rescuing Elizabeth than he would without it.

Thomas nodded and said, "Thank you." Then he turned to the coachman and gave him the directions for the port from which Dalwood had said Merlion meant to sail.

Inside the carriage, Rivendale spoke quietly. "I hope we are in time."

There was no need for Thomas or Sir Robert to say aloud how fervently they agreed. As the carriage began to race toward the coast, Thomas began to speak. "I did not betray Anna Dalwood. Except to refuse to marry her when my father pressed me to do so. It was someone else who did what Dalwood lays at my door."

"We did not take his words to be truth," Rivendale said quietly. "I, at any rate, have known you too long to believe you capable of such behavior."

"What did he mean about Elizabeth taking in sewing?" Thomas persisted. "Do either of you know?"

Both men shook their heads.

"I think that is something you will have to ask her yourself," Stamford said gently. He paused, and then added, "Even if she did take in sewing while you were gone, I doubt she did anything worse. And while some of the *ton* might sneer at her for doing so, I should rather admire her ingenuity and her determination to manage, one way or another."

"But why didn't she tell me?"

"I suppose that is another thing only she can tell you," Rivendale said, echoing Stamford's advice.

The boat rocked abominably and if she had not been so determined to show an impassive face to her captors, Lisbeth would have been ill. As it was, her anger sustained her. And anger was easier to accept than fear.

But she was afraid. She was afraid for herself, but even more she was afraid for Thomas. She also worried what her son, Tom, must be thinking. It would be the first time in his short life that she had not been there to kiss him good night, the first night she would not be there if he had trouble breathing. What would he think when she didn't come to tuck him in? What would he think if she never came back at all?

Lisbeth was a realist. She knew her chances for living through the next few days or weeks were slight. And even if her captor did not kill her, how was she ever to get home? Particularly once they landed in France? Even if she got free, it might not be easy for an Englishwoman to book passage home. Nor did she have the funds to do so, even if she could find a ship willing to take her.

Another woman might have cried. Lisbeth looked for ways to make her captor's existence more miserable. It wasn't particularly difficult. He obviously had orders to keep her alive and in good condition. Either that, or it was something his plans required. In any event, he gritted his teeth and complied each time she told him she needed privacy to use the chamber pot. When she claimed to be faint from hunger, he sent one of the men to fetch her food.

It was not that Lisbeth wished to eat. Indeed, it wasn't easy for her to do so. Each bite had to be choked down. But it both annoyed her captor and it would give her strength should the opportunity occur for escape. And no matter how long the odds, if the chance came, Lisbeth meant to take it.

So she smiled and ate and pretended to a calm she did not feel. She watched her captors, all of them, to try to discover which one might be the weakest. She watched for what made them angry and what made them bored.

Perhaps, she thought, she ought to have played the role of a helpless, fainting, poor-spirited female. But it had not occurred to her to do so until she had already established that she was quite the opposite. Still, she wondered if perhaps she should begin to let them think her cowed. Perhaps then they would lower their guard?

No. Her reaction was immediate and certain. There was a look in the eyes of the Frenchman that told Lisbeth he liked to frighten people. If she seemed cowed, he would only press her further. If she stood up to him, he would spend his time trying to think of a way to alter her attitude, but he would do nothing that he did not think would succeed.

So Lisbeth dabbed daintily at her lips with the napkin she had demanded, and pushed aside the empty plate. She noted the way the other two men looked jealous and wondered how long it had been since they had been allowed to partake of a meal. Was it possible, she wondered, to use their resentment against their leader?

It was, she decided, a thought worth pursuing. She touched the locket at her throat for courage. And then, aloud she said in a languid voice, "I am finished. You may take this refuse away."

"You are very particular for a woman in your circumstance," her captor said, leaning over her in what he obviously wished to be a threatening way.

Lisbeth merely raised her eyebrows and allowed a faint look of hauteur to cross her face. "Woman? I am not a woman, sir. I am a lady. And I will thank you to remember that. As for being particular, is there any reason

I should lower my standards simply because I am subject to the whims of my inferiors?"

That caused his face to darken, as she hoped it would. "You do not seem to grasp the true nature of your situation!" he snapped.

She smiled. "I grasp very well that you mean to murder me and that you hope to do the same to my husband. I see no reason to allow my last few hours or days or weeks to be ruled by fear. It would be an appalling waste of time."

He stared at her as if he thought her mad, or as if he doubted the evidence of his own ears. "You are impossible!" he said at last.

Lisbeth smiled sweetly. "That is certainly my dearest wish," she said.

He turned his back on her. She risked a glance at the other two men. They were looking at each other and rolling their eyes. They could not imagine what to make of her either, and that was all to the good. The more she could keep them feeling as if they were in Bedlam, the better her chances might be to disrupt their plans.

It was an odd thing, but her greatest fear was not for herself, it was for Thomas. What would happen to him if he came after her? And what could he possibly have done to provoke such a strong desire for revenge? If she knew, perhaps she could use it to advantage?

With that notion in mind, Lisbeth began her campaign. "I cannot see," she said with a pretend yawn, "why on earth you should wish to lure my husband to you. He is a dear creature but sadly dull."

"Not nearly so dull as you think," her captor said with a smirk.

"Yes, but . . ." Lisbeth began. She frowned, and then shrugged. She spoke as though she were entirely bewildered. "Very well, perhaps he is not so dull around other men. But he seems the most amiable fellow alive. How could he possibly have made an enemy of you—as he so evidently has done?"

"Our respective countries made us enemies," the fellow replied.

She frowned again and looked at her captor with wide eyes. "Yes, but the war is over and your anger seems more than that," she said slowly, as though pondering out the matter. "Indeed, if you did not tell me it was impersonal, I should have thought you had taken a vow of vengeance against my husband."

He drew his breath in with a hiss. "I did not say it was not personal," he told her with a snarl. "It is very personal! But the original dispute grew out of the war between our two countries. And for some of us, the war will never be over."

Lisbeth pretended to a sigh of exasperation. "Yes, yes, I know—he was a prisoner of war. I collect you must have been one of his guards. But I still do not see why that should make you so angry at him—even if he did escape."

"I was not his guard!" Unlike Lisbeth, her captor's exasperation was genuine. He leaned forward. "Didn't your husband tell you? He wasn't a prisoner of war for very long. You're quite correct that he escaped, but I was not then in charge of his prison. No, his path crossed mine when he chose to steal documents to take them back to your Wellington. I caught him twice, and each time he escaped. One of those times cost me my wife."

"Your wife!" Lisbeth did not have to pretend to be dismayed. Still, she rallied. "I cannot believe my husband would have hurt any woman."

"He did not directly hurt her," the Frenchman admitted reluctantly. "But it was as we were trying to recapture him that she was shot. So, you see, her death was his fault. It should lay heavy upon his conscience. Particularly since she was kind to him."

He paused for several moments, as though he could

not bear to continue. But he did. His voice became harsh as he went on. "She was kinder to Kepley than she ought to have been. Oh, don't worry, my dear. I do not mean that anything improper occurred. We were too happy together for that. But my wife had a kind heart and she worried over the prisoners that, on rare occasions, she encountered. She had come to my office, that day, to bring me something to eat. And your husband spoke to her gently so that she did not see what a serpent he was. She died because of that, and I shall never forgive your husband for being the cause."

"And that is why," Lisbeth said slowly, "I am the perfect bait for you to use. That is why my death will be the perfect revenge."

Her captor frowned. "I hope it may not come to that. I will be happy if I simply have your husband in my hands again. I cannot simply let you go home, it is true. And I do not know what those who are with me in this will wish to do with you, but it is possible you will be kept alive."

Lisbeth had to fight the leap of hope that rose in her breast, for she was very much afraid that such a possibility would only come at the cost of Thomas's life. Still, she had to ask.

"And my husband?" Lisbeth said. "Will he be permitted to live as well?"

Her captor's expression hardened. "No. There is no chance Kepley will be allowed to live." When she started to protest, the Frenchman held up a hand to forestall her. His voice was harsh as he said, "No! Do not ask me again! His fate is determined, but yours, *madame* is still in doubt. At least allow yourself that hope. Do not force me to determine on your death as well."

Lisbeth fell silent. He meant what he said; she could read it in the expression on his face, the stance of his body, the sound of his voice. She had pushed him as far as he could be pushed. Now it was time to fall silent and plan.

Chapter 17

Kepley, Stamford, and Rivendale stood on the deck of the small boat. They were shortly to transfer to one that was even smaller. It was not a pleasant thought, given the height of the waves. An even worse thought was the knowledge that Elizabeth was in the hands of Jean Merlion. Knowledge confirmed by someone who had seen Elizabeth bundled aboard a ship with him not two hours before.

What they intended to do was dangerous, but far less dangerous than waiting until their quarry landed in France—for that was where they were certain he was headed. Ah, there was the boat they were watching for.

What looked to be a crew of the most appalling ruffians helped them aboard. Thomas greeted some of them by name, knowing them to be men dedicated to the good of England. What surprised him was that Stamford greeted some of them by name as well. When he cocked an inquiring look at Stamford the other man merely shrugged and grinned.

"I haven't always been a gentleman," Stamford said.

Neither Rivendale nor Thomas questioned him. The need for silence from this point out was too apparent to all of them. Swiftly, however, Thomas outlined their situation to the men in the boat.

"A small boat shipped out about two hours ago. We need to find and board it. It's headed to France, and we need to do so before she gets there." He paused then added, "My wife is on board."

The captain of this even smaller boat nodded. "We passed her a short time ago. She's moving slowly and we should have no trouble catching up to her."

There was no need to say anything more. As much as these men looked like ruffians, they were not. They needed little direction to do their jobs and do them well. If they said they could catch up with the boat ahead, then they could. And Thomas knew he could depend on them to help rescue Elizabeth.

Miss Winsham was not pleased. She was not pleased to find herself at dinner alone with Lord and Lady Aylsham, neither of whom seemed particularly delighted to have to eat alone with her. She was not pleased when Elizabeth had not returned by the time Tom was to be put to bed.

Tom was even less pleased. He signified his displeasure by crying inconsolably. And that led to an attack of difficult breathing as anyone—and particularly Elizabeth—must have known it would.

Margaret Winsham was not downstairs to see when Lord Thomas came back to the town house and was given a note to read. She did not know he left again straight after. All she knew was that Elizabeth was not there and her son needed her.

For once, Margaret's efforts to ease Tom's breathing did not work. Indeed, his breathing only became more and more labored, despite the herbs, despite the pot of boiling water inside the tent. With growing alarm, Margaret sent for Dr. Brooks.

He made her feel as shy and awkward as a schoolgirl. And there were times he infuriated her with his attitude toward her sex. But there was also something about the man that claimed her trust. Indeed, at the moment, she didn't know whom else to ask for help. Not about this. For all that he had disparaged her use of herbs at the start, Dr. Brooks had come to respect her understanding of them. He had said so just this morning and even confided in her some rather unorthodox notions of his own. Perhaps he could help Tom now.

Miss Winsham did not know if Dr. Brooks would come. She did not even know if he could be found, for it would not be at all surprising if he had gone out this evening, as gentlemen so regularly did. But she sent for him nonetheless.

He had not yet arrived when Lady Aylsham appeared in the nursery. She clutched at her throat as she watched Margaret struggle to calm the child. "What is wrong with Tom, Miss Winsham?" she asked.

In short, terse sentences, Margaret explained. Then she paused, looked directly at the marchioness and said, bluntly, "Why do you ask me about the child when you do not even believe he is your grandson?"

Lady Aylsham came closer. "He reminds me of my little brother. He, too, had trouble breathing. Tom is fortunate to have you to help him."

Margaret shook her head. "I am not of much help tonight. Where is Dr. Brooks? I had hoped he would be here by now!"

Even as she spoke the words, Dr. Brooks was shown into the nursery. He muttered something disparaging about majordomos who answered doors and could not distinguish between a man who was a doctor coming to pay a social call and a physician on his way to treat a patient. But whatever obstacle he had encountered, Dr. Brooks had bullied his way through.

It was a comforting thought. Margaret only hoped he could bully his way through the obstacle of Tom's increasing discomfort and somehow find a way to help the child. In her quiet, efficient way, ignoring Lady Aylsham who seemed strangely reluctant to leave the nursery, she told him about Tom's latest attack.

Brooks was brisk and efficient, but gentle with the child. The questions he put to Margaret were those she would have asked had she stood in his shoes. If the physician was worried, he did not show it in his expression. He was cheerful and teased Tom easily, as if they had not a care in the world. Under this attention, the child seemed to calm a bit, and as a result his breathing seemed to ease just a trifle.

In the end, the doctor even held Tom's hand until the child fell asleep. Then they both slipped quietly out of the nursery with orders for the nursery maid to call Margaret at once should he wake and suffer a relapse.

"Are you coming?" Margaret asked Lady Aylsham.

The marchioness shook her head. "I shall stay with him a little longer, I think."

Margaret hesitated, then shrugged. "As you will."

Outside in the hallway, Dr. Brooks stopped. "I wish you to bring him to see me tomorrow, Miss Winsham," he said. "Your niece's locket put me in mind of a book I have that may suggest a way to treat the boy. I shall be interested to see what you think. I may even be able to prepare a tea or a tonic or something that will ease his distress in situations like this. At the very least I think I may be able to offer you something to help him sleep that is far safer than giving the boy laudanum."

Margaret nodded. "I am certain his mother and father will wish to bring him."

"No!" Brooks said sharply. At her startled look he added, "That is to say, they may come as well, of course, but I believe it to be important for you to be there. You are the one who has, in effect, been treating the boy up until now and your input will be invaluable."

"Very well. I shall come," she said primly.

He chuckled. "Now don't poker up like that, Miss Winsham! It isn't simply your experience and wisdom I wish to consult." He paused and his voice took on an entirely different tone as he said, softly, "I am foolish enough to wish for every possible opportunity to see you and to hear your voice."

As he spoke, the physician started to reach toward Margaret. She had the oddest notion that he meant to touch her cheek. But a nearby sound startled them and they both turned a fiery red.

Brooks hastily stepped back and cleared his throat. "Yes, well, er, I had better go. I shall see you tomorrow, Miss Winsham!"

And then he fled. Margaret could only watch him go, frozen where she stood. He had touched her heart by showing her a kindness, a gentleness no man had ever shown her before. And he had treated Tom with that same kindness and gentleness. That had gotten past her defenses in a way she had not known to be possible.

Yes, she would take the child to see Dr. Brooks tomorrow. Just let Kepley or Elizabeth try to stop her from coming along! she thought fiercely. But then her spirits sagged as she realized again that they could not yet be home. For if they had returned, she could not imagine that the servants would not have sent them straight up to the nursery.

With a sigh, Margaret turned to go back into the nursery herself. She paused in the doorway, stunned at the sight of Lady Aylsham softly singing a lullaby to little Tom. Whatever the reason, something had softened the marchioness's heart toward her grandson and Margaret was not about to intrude.

They were almost together. The men in the small boat drew alongside the larger one in dead silence. The men aboard the larger boat were clearly bored, for they did not even notice as first one man and then another climbed silently aboard. They had been watching out for naval ships but nothing the size of the boat that carried Kepley, Stamford, and Rivendale.

Still, the men took nothing for granted. They continued to move in silence as they spread out over the boat, rendering unconscious any crewman they could find. They might have made their way unseen to the cabins and found Elizabeth, but suddenly their fortune turned. Someone, coming up from belowdecks, caught sight of the intruders and shouted out a cry of alarm. He was swiftly silenced, but not swiftly enough.

By the time they had dealt with the sailors roused by the warning, Thomas knew Elizabeth's captors would be on guard and waiting for them. He, Stamford, and Rivendale made their way carefully toward the cabin where a seaman had been persuaded to tell them she was being held. But it was Thomas alone who rapped on the door.

"Come in. You will find the door unbarred," a familiar voice called out.

So it was the man Thomas feared. He took a deep breath and stepped inside the cabin, leaving the door open just a notch behind him.

"Monsieur Merlion," he said politely.

"Lord Thomas. Welcome. I had not expected to see you quite so soon. I admit you have surprised me. Your presence here means I must assume this ship has been successfully boarded by Englishmen."

Thomas nodded. And then he waited for Merlion to speak again. He could not gauge the man's mood, but since the fellow held a knife to Elizabeth's throat, he wanted to do nothing that would startle or anger him.

"You may have my ship, but I have your wife," the Frenchman said, a hint of madness in his eyes. "Come no closer! You are quick, I know, but even so, you could not hope to rescue her before I slit her throat."

Thomas understood that madness. Had the tables been reversed and it had been Elizabeth who had died three months ago, he, too, would have been half mad with grief and wanting revenge. He had to make Jean Merlion believe that harming Elizabeth would not give it to him. But God only knew if the trick would work. Still he could think of nothing else to try. Nothing that might have any chance of success and leave her unharmed, at any rate.

Thomas took a deep breath. Then he shrugged. "Do it," he said in a weary voice. "You will save me a great deal of trouble and annoyance if you do."

Merlion started and a thin trickle of blood appeared at Elizabeth's throat. Thomas held himself very still. He forced himself to pretend not to care. He even made himself pretend to smile at the sight. And he made certain he did not flinch at the Frenchman's next words.

"You are playing a game with me! Well, me, I do not believe you!" Monsieur Merlion snarled.

Thomas shrugged again. The man looked puzzled. "I have seen you," he said. "The oh, so devoted couple. Now you pretend you do not care? Bah! It is incredible."

Now Thomas allowed himself to smile, and it was not a pleasant smile. He looked at Elizabeth with contempt. "Indeed? But you see, I do despise her. What man would not despise the wife who cuckolded him?"

"No, no," Merlion said, shaking his head. "I have *seen* you together—in the park!"

Thomas tilted back his head and let his smile broaden. He willed his shoulders to relax and his body to express complete carelessness. "Ah, yes, the park. Tell me, sir. If you came home to find *your* wife had slept with other men, and even meant to foist one of their by-blows off as *your* son, what would you do?"

"She would not have done such a thing!"

"But if she did?" Thomas asked in a voice that was silky soft and dangerous. When the Frenchman did not answer, he went on, in the same tone as before. "That is precisely what Lady Thomas has done to me, you see. And I suppose I could have cast her off. But then all the rumors would have been confirmed and I would have looked the fool. Better to beat my wife in private and in public force her to pretend we are besotted with each other. Even her former lovers do not know the truth. They think she has tired of them."

Thomas ended with a soft, cruel laugh. Merlion stared at him, then down at Elizabeth, who was also staring at Thomas and cowering as if he terrified her.

Everything depended upon the next few minutes. The Frenchman clearly did not know what to think. The other two men in the cabin were no threat—they stood behind Merlion and were more interested in the byplay of words than in Elizabeth. They would simply do as they were told.

The Frenchman seemed to make up his mind. "So you do not care what I do with her?" he said.

Thomas shrugged. He looked down at his nails. He glared at Elizabeth with eyes as hard as coal. Then he looked again at Merlion, biting off each word as he spoke.

"If you rid me of a bride I have come to despise, then I shall be in your debt. I shall say that you attacked her just as I was trying to rescue her. I know I will be believed. If you don't rid me of her, well, she shall have all that much more reason to fear me when I take her home. I do not think she will dare humiliate me again."

"You are very confident!" Merlion said.

"My men control the ship."

"And if I kill you?"

"You might find that hard—"

Thomas got no farther before suddenly Elizabeth moved. She took the Frenchman by surprise. She shoved Merlion so hard that he went sprawling sideways and the knife flew from his hand. Instantly knives appeared in the hands of the other two men, even as a knife appeared in Thomas's. Elizabeth scrambled on her knees and had the Frenchman's knife before he could retrieve it. She held it pointed toward him in a manner that left no doubt she meant to use it.

Merlion scrambled back, reading something in her face that frightened him. At the same moment, the other two men rushed forward and Elizabeth stumbled back against Thomas. Behind him, the cabin door burst open and both Stamford and Rivendale leveled pistols on the men.

"I believe," Thomas said carefully to Merlion, "that this round is mine. Go home. I know you will not believe me, and I doubt it will matter to you, but I did not wish for your wife to die."

"You are right," Merlion said. "It does not matter to me what you meant or did not mean to happen. My wife, she is dead, and I will never forgive you for that."

It would have been wiser to wait for another chance for revenge. It would have been wiser to go home and simply grieve. It would even have been wiser to wait until they left the cabin and thought themselves safe from attack. But there was a madness in the Frenchman's soul and suddenly he could not bear it any longer.

He shouted curses at both Thomas and Lisbeth. And then, when that did not provoke them, he lunged for Thomas and two shots rang out—one from each of the pistols held by Stamford and Rivendale. Merlion crumpled to the floor.

Elizabeth immediately bent over him and so did Thomas. She looked at him and he shook his head. "He is dead. Perhaps it is kinder this way, though I would not have chosen such an end to all of this."

"It is just as well," Stamford said with a sober expression. "Otherwise both of you would have forever been looking over your shoulders. Had he stopped to consider the matter, Monsieur Merlion might have realized that would have been sufficient revenge even if he never tried to act against you again."

"What's done is done," Rivendale added softly. "It is time we were on our way."

Kepley nodded and helped Elizabeth to her feet. Stamford, Rivendale, Thomas, and Elizabeth were soon back in the small boat, headed for shore and home.

Chapter 18

It was past dawn before a very bedraggled Thomas and Elizabeth mounted the steps of the London town house. The servants were already at their morning duties and any number of curious and alarmed looks followed their progress into the house and up the stairs to their suite of rooms.

There had not been any privacy in which to talk. Stamford and Rivendale had insisted on setting the Kepleys down first, so that when they reached their bedchamber, they thought they would be alone together for the first time since they had parted company in the park. They were mistaken.

"Sir! May I say what a relief it is to have you home again? The staff has been most concerned," George, Thomas's batman, greeted them at their bedroom door.

"Oh, ma'am, we're that happy to see you safe and sound, we are!" Lisbeth's maid added, not to be outdone.

Nor would either servant agree to be dismissed. "After the night you've most obviously had? I should think not, sir!" George said, in shocked accents. "As it is, sir, I think that coat, as well as the rest of your attire, must be considered a dead loss."

"And your riding habit, ma'am! It's ruined! Whatever will you do until you can have a new one made up?" Lisbeth's maid chimed in.

"She shan't be getting another riding habit," Thomas said, ruthlessly cutting short George's next exclamation.

Three pairs of eyes stared at him. "I'm not?" Lisbeth asked, her voice not altogether steady.

"No, you are not," Thomas answered, his voice firm.

"But, sir, why not?" the maid could not help but ask.

A glare from George informed her of the solecism she had committed and caused her to clamp shut her lips before she could commit another. Only then did the batman turn to Thomas and say in a careless voice, "No doubt you have your reasons, sir. But I take leave to say that I think perhaps I may know a trick or two that will salvage madam's habit."

"No. Burn it!" Thomas retorted.

Lisbeth looked at him warily, as if she thought he might have lost his wits. Until he smiled, and then she knew that whatever his reasons, it would be all right.

They allowed themselves to be shepherded into separate rooms to undress. Indeed, Lisbeth was so tired that she found it almost a comfort to have someone else lift the habit off over her head and slip on a soft night shift in its stead. She also found soothing the feel of her maid pulling the few remaining pins out of her hair and then brushing it until it gleamed. And by then it was time to climb into bed, no candle needed in the morning light.

To be sure, it was a bit disconcerting to have so interested an audience as George and the maid, but finally they had been persuaded to leave the room and to inform the other servants that no one was to disturb the couple until one or both chose to come downstairs.

And then, at last, Thomas and Lisbeth found themselves alone together. For several very long moments they simply stared at each other. In the end, she spoke first.

"Why did you say they ought to burn my riding habit?" Lisbeth asked.

"Why didn't you tell me you were frightened of horses?" Thomas replied. "Had I known, I would never have pressed you to ride."

"Wouldn't you?" she countered. "Wouldn't you have tried to help me past my fear?"

He flushed. "Well, perhaps. But I shan't make that mistake now. Whatever you wish or don't wish to do is acceptable to me."

"I see."

He sighed. "I only acted as I did because of my fears. With Jean Merlion's death all that is at an end. But what the devil were you doing riding off with Dalwood? I was terrified when I couldn't find you!"

"I simply backed away, thinking to wait for you in the shade of a tree," Lisbeth said slowly. "I suddenly felt unaccountably faint. Lord Peter saw me and rode over to offer to escort me back here. He said you would understand. Instead I found myself being dragged into a carriage and bundled off to the coast, where I was forced onto the boat with that Frenchman."

"Dalwood and Merlion must have been watching for just such an opportunity," Thomas said, his voice grim. "At first I thought you were angry at me and were simply determined to teach me a lesson by making me worry where you had gone. Then, when I found that letter waiting for me here, signed by Merlion, my heart was in my throat that I might lose you. And after I spoke with Dalwood, I was more afraid than ever."

"You cannot know the relief I felt when I realized you had come to rescue me!" she answered.

"No?" he teased. "It cannot have been any greater than mine when I knew we would reach the boat before she landed in France."

As though she caught his mood, Lisbeth began to tease him. With mock severity she said, "I did not, however, appreciate you telling that Frenchman that you would be grateful if he removed the nuisance of a wife you had!"

Thomas pretended to look mournful. "But then I could have been a carefree bachelor again."

Lisbeth pretended to glare at him and he pulled her

close into his arms and kissed the top of her head. "I could not think what else to say," he told her, his voice scarcely above a whisper. "I could not think what else to do but to try to catch him off guard and disconcert his expectations."

In spite of herself, Lisbeth chuckled. "We seem to think alike, for I did the very same thing."

He looked at her, and his eyes were alight with mischief. "So I concluded," he said, "from the intricacies of the curses he flung at both our heads. Did you really tell him you found his threats boring?"

"No," Lisbeth said in a deceptively meek voice. "I told him they would make me angry. And I told him he had to feed me. And I told him he had to give me privacy to use the chamber pot. And when he said he disliked me, I told him he would dislike me a great deal more before we were done."

Thomas could not help himself—he laughed and pulled Lisbeth even closer. "I knew we were well suited," he told her. "I said so when I asked you to marry me and I was quite right, wasn't I?"

That, however, reminded Lisbeth of a grievance she still had. "Where were you those twenty months?" she asked. "And do not say you were a prisoner of war, for the Frenchman told me that was only for a very short time. He said the two of you encountered each other more than once. So what were you doing? And why didn't you come home?"

He answered the last question first. "I couldn't," he said. "I was needed there, in France, to find out what others could not." He sighed. "If only I had known the straits to which you were reduced—but I did not. I had no contact with England until Napoleon surrendered and I was given leave to come back home. It was only then I realized how deserted you must have felt, how difficult your situation was."

Lisbeth didn't want to ask the next question, but she

felt she had to know and that, perhaps, he had to say. "He said you were the cause of his wife's death."

"That is the thing I regret most," Thomas said. "I did not mean for it to happen. No one did. But she distracted him for a moment. Long enough for me to attempt my escape. The information I carried was important and urgently needed back home. So when she distracted him, I ran. The guards fired just as she turned and stepped into the path of their guns. If they had not shot her, they might have shot me. Her death saved my life. But I didn't know she had been killed, not until I heard some soldiers talking as they searched for me below the spot in which I was hiding."

Lisbeth considered for some moments the things he had said. Then, slowly, reluctantly she said, "I thought you were a soldier, not a spy."

"I never meant to become a spy," Thomas said. "But that was how I was needed most, how I could save the most lives, and I could not refuse. I did not mean, did not expect, that what I did would ever put you in danger. And for that I shall never forgive myself."

"If you had told me about this Merlion, perhaps I would have been on guard," Lisbeth said quietly.

Thomas nodded, conceding the point. Even so, he tried to explain. "At first I thought I must be mistaken. He haunted my dreams and I thought perhaps he had begun to haunt my days as well. That it was all my imagination."

He paused and had to force himself to go on, had to force himself to meet her eyes. "To tell you about Jean Merlion," he said, his voice softly pleading, "I would have had to tell you the rest. It would have meant having you know what I did. I would have had to tell you about his wife. I would have had to talk about things I have tried very hard to forget. All I could think to do was to try to make certain you always had someone by your side when you went out. And that, whenever possible, that someone was me."

"And if I had asked you why you were so determined that I should not go out alone, instead of simply kicking up a fuss," she said slowly, "perhaps you would have found the courage to tell me."

"I hope that I would have done so," Thomas replied. He waited a moment and then he said, his voice stronger now, "I was not the only one with secrets. If you had told me you were afraid of horses, I would never have forced you to ride and you would not have been vulnerable to Dalwood luring you from my side because you felt ill."

"I did not want to disappoint you," Lisbeth said, her own voice a plea now. "You seemed so much to want me to ride with you, and it even pleased your parents. I thought that I might overcome my fear and then you need never know."

He nodded, but he was not yet done. "There is another secret," he said quietly. "When Stamford, Rivendale, and I went to see Dalwood, to make him tell us where you had gone, he said that you had been earning money by taking in sewing while I was gone. I suppose that is why Mrs. Parker was there that first day I came home, not because you were ordering new gowns for yourself?"

Lisbeth's chin came up in unconscious defiance at the censure she thought she heard in his voice. She met his gaze steadily as she said, "Yes. What else was I to do? If I had not taken in sewing, there were times we would have had no food upon the table. I put off repairs on the house. I mended my old gowns. I did not purchase anything except what I absolutely had to. So I ask you, what else was I to do?"

He closed his eyes a moment. "One more sin to be laid at my door," he said softly, as though to himself. To Lisbeth he said, "I do not blame you. I just wonder why you didn't tell me."

Lisbeth looked at him, her lower lip trembling as she

remembered the months he was gone, the fears that had driven her. "Do you really wonder?" she answered softly. "When your parents had told me, more than once, that in marrying me you had married far beneath you? When they talked of bloodlines and consequence? How could I give them, how could I give you, one more reason to disdain me?"

"Oh, Elizabeth!" he said, pulling her into his arms, her face against his chest, one hand cradling the back of her head. "I should never have thought such a thing!"

"No?" she asked, pulling back to study his face. "Perhaps not. But I was so afraid. You had finally come home, Thomas, but you seemed so angry with me already. You seemed so disappointed in what you found that I could not bear to disappoint you further!"

Thomas took her chin and tilted it so that she had to look into his eyes. "I was never and shall never, I could never, be disappointed in you, Elizabeth," he said. "We have both made mistakes, but I have always known that the best thing I ever did was to marry you. And nothing you tell me could ever change that! If I have ever had any doubts, it was as to whether I was good enough for you."

Lisbeth stared back, wanting to believe him. There had never been a time in her life when she didn't feel she had disappointed those around her. Was it truly going to be different with Thomas? Something in his eyes told her that it was and in the end, she gave a tiny cry and threw her arms around his neck. He smiled, and that gave her courage.

"No more distance between us," Lisbeth said, her voice pleading. "No more secrets or lies. No more hiding what we most fear. Please? I should like us to be a shelter for each other. The one place where we may truly be ourselves."

He had no words to answer her. Instead, Thomas took her hand and kissed her fingertips, one by one. And then he proceeded to show Elizabeth just how much her words had meant to him.

Miss Winsham tapped her foot impatiently. Whatever was she to do? She did not feel quite right about taking Tom to see Dr. Brooks without either Kepley or Elizabeth present. And she certainly did not feel comfortable doing so without their permission. But the servants had informed her, quite haughtily, that the couple was not to be disturbed, not even by Margaret, not even for Tom.

Margaret hesitated. She was not at all certain that Elizabeth had truly meant all of that. She must have simply been too tired to think of those exceptions. Nonetheless, it was clear to Miss Winsham that the servants meant to do as asked and might very well try to stop her if she went and rapped on their door herself.

But what was she to do? Dr. Brooks was expecting them and Margaret could not disappoint him. Not after he had been so kind as to come last night. Not when she thought he might have a way to help Tom.

Miss Winsham waited a few minutes longer and then she came to a decision. She would take Tom to see the doctor herself. After all, as Dr. Brooks had said, she knew the child's health as well as anyone. She had supervised his treatment all this time.

Miss Winsham swept up to the nursery. There she spent half an hour intimidating the nursery maid into agreeing to allow her to take Tom out of the house. As she left the room with the child, she could hear the angry mutterings behind her.

"Something is very wrong in this house, it is! First the young mistress yesterday, and then the young master, and now the baby. A disgrace it is! Positively a disgrace. I've more than half a mind to tender my resignation, I do."

A soft voice answered her and while Margaret could not hear what the girl said, she did hear the nursery maid's reply. "Well, of course I'm not really going to abandon the boy! I'm only talking, I am. A pretty thing if I was to give up my charge every time one of the parents or aunts or uncles or such takes a foolish notion into their heads! No, I'll talk to his lordship or her ladyship later; that's what I'll do. They'll set Miss Winsham straight. You won't see no more of this nonsense again after that."

Miss Winsham smiled grimly to herself. She would like to see the nursery maid telling Elizabeth that she did not know what to do. She would like to be there to hear the complaints. And perhaps she would be, for there was no telling how long Kepley and Elizabeth would sleep. The servants said they had not returned until after dawn. But for now, she was off to see Dr. Brooks. And she hoped that he might have the answers she and Elizabeth had thus far been unable to find.

When the carriage pulled up at the physician's town house, Margaret found it absurdly gratifying to discover that Dr. Brooks was waiting for her. He had said, yesterday, when they parted, that he would be, but she had thought it no more than a figure of speech. And yet, indeed, he opened the door to her and Tom himself. To be sure, he looked a trifle taken aback when he realized that neither Kepley nor Elizabeth had accompanied her, but he recovered himself quickly.

"Come in. Come in. Right into this room over here. I keep my office on the ground floor so that my patients need not climb any stairs. Here, please set him down on this table and let me examine the poor fellow."

Tom did not take kindly to this examination. Nor to the absence of both his parents. He kept asking for his mother. It was only one more thing to like about the doctor, Margaret thought, that he was not in the least disconcerted by Tom's screams. Indeed he seemed almost pleased at how loud the child was able to yell.

"Means the lungs are strong," he said, "and that must always be a concern with an illness like this."

Her own emotions on tenterhooks, Margaret could not help but press Dr. Brooks to tell her what he thought. "Well? Can you help him?" she asked. "You mentioned a book last night and a tonic that might be of help? Do you still think so? What goes into the tonic and why have no other doctors suggested it before now?"

He did not at once answer, but handed Tom back to her. Then he merely said, "Come upstairs to the drawing room with me, Miss Winsham. I have arranged for some tea to be brewed and a plate of pastries set out. That will please Tom and we may talk."

Margaret followed him, for she did not see what other choice she might have, but she did so most impatiently.

Chapter 19

As promised, there were treats that Tom was happy enough to occupy himself with eating. And that left Miss Winsham and Dr. Brooks free to talk. Except that they did not at once talk about the child.

Dr. Brooks asked one of the maids to take charge of Tom and she was able to coax him off into a corner to play. Margaret expected the doctor to immediately launch into an explanation of the child's condition and what he thought the prognosis might be. Instead, he asked her if she would like to see his town house.

Mystified, but presuming the man had a reason, she agreed. It was a small house, but neatly appointed. With so much space given over to the rooms where he saw patients or prepared their medicines, the rest of the space had to be used with utmost efficiency—and it was.

He did not show her the bedrooms, of course, but she imagined they were much the same. If there was a fault to be found in the house, it was that it was so spartanly furnished. As though he read her thoughts, Dr. Brooks said apologetically, "I suppose some would say it needs a woman's touch. But I've never found quite the right woman."

Margaret nodded, not quite certain what one could say to that. But the physician seemed to know what he wished to say. He pressed on.

"And I suppose I may presume that you have never

found quite the right man, or you would not still be unwed either, Miss Winsham."

Margaret thought for a moment of the face she had seen in the locket. She could not know it, but her face took on a wistful expression. "No," she said softly, "I have not found the man I was meant to marry."

"Do you think that you ever will?" Dr. Brooks asked diffidently.

Now what was one to say to that? Margaret asked herself indignantly. Particularly when the only man who had ever tempted her was the one who had just posed the question?

As though he understood her reluctance, particularly when he had asked her as they were standing in the hallway, Dr. Brooks opened one more door. "Perhaps we would be more comfortable in my study," he said. "I have the book I told you about on my desk."

She nodded. Anything to put off, at least for a few more moments, answering his question! And Margaret had no doubt that he meant to have an answer. Dr. Brooks had that determined look in his eyes that she had come to recognize as common to men bent on a quest. Though why on earth her views on marriage should matter to him was something she dared not allow herself to ponder.

Besides, Margaret told herself, she truly did wish to see that book. So intent was she on doing so, that she noticed nothing else but the tome on Brooks's desk. He held it up and she caught her breath. There, on the cover, was a design that looked a great deal like the one on their family locket. Instinctively Margaret's hand went to her throat, but of course the locket was no longer there, it belonged now to Elizabeth.

Dr. Brooks did not appear to notice. Already he was opening the book to show her the relevant pages. "You see?" he asked triumphantly. "A recipe very similar to yours. But you see how they have added an herb or two that I would not have thought of combining with the others. I took the liberty of making up a tea from these herbs and I am preparing a tonic as well. That, of course, will need some number of days to be ready. But for now, we could try the tea."

He held out the book to her and Margaret took it gingerly. One hand stroked the pages and for the first time she felt truly avaricious for a possession. She looked at the page he had mentioned, but then could not resist glancing through the rest of the book as well.

"How I wish I had such a book!" she said softly. "I do not suppose you know if there are other copies to be purchased anywhere?"

Dr. Brooks hesitated and cleared his throat. "I, er, well, I had some thoughts on that, Miss Winsham. Please, won't you sit down?"

Mystified, Margaret moved toward the chair he indicated, the book still clasped in her hands. When she was seated, he cleared his throat again. But she scarcely heard him for her eyes were fixed on the portrait that stared back at her from above his shoulder. It hung over the fireplace and suddenly all thoughts of the book or tonics or even Tom were forgotten.

"W-who is that?" she asked, her voice scarcely louder than a whisper.

Dr. Brooks frowned. It was his turn to be mystified. He pivoted, looked at the painting, and smiled. "That was me, in my salad days. A long time ago, I'm afraid. It was said to be a very good likeness. Why do you ask?"

Margaret rose to her feet and moved forward, as though mesmerized, until she stood directly before the painting. She reached out and touched the frame. Over her shoulder she asked, her voice full of constraint, "When was it painted? What year, I mean?"

Dr. Brooks told her. In a way, she was not surprised to hear that it had been painted the year before she moved into the woods. The year she had looked into the locket. She turned and stared at Dr. Brooks. Here and there, particularly about the eyes, Margaret could see that he was the same man and she wondered that she had not seen it before.

She would have reached out and touched his face, but that would have been foolish beyond permission. Margaret clasped her hands behind her back instead. Her face was very pale, so much so that she realized the physician was looking at her with great alarm.

"Miss Winsham? Are you all right, Miss Winsham? Perhaps you should sit down. Are you feeling faint? Do you have smelling salts with you?"

That roused her and abruptly she was herself again. "I never carry the awful stuff!" Margaret snapped at him. "I don't need smelling salts and if someone else is so foolish as to go about fainting, let 'em carry their own!"

Dr. Brooks breathed a sigh of relief. "Now you sound more like yourself," he said. "But you gave me quite a turn. Is something the matter?"

Margaret stared at him. How could she tell him that she had just discovered he was the man whose face she once thought she saw in a locket? How could she tell him that, if he was, he was the man she was supposed to marry? It sounded fantastic to her; how much more so would it sound to him? If he did not clap her up in Bedlam, he would most certainly decide he ought to put a distance between them and that was something she did not think she could bear.

So now she smiled brightly and said, "I am quite recovered, Dr. Brooks, I assure you. I think it is just worry over my niece and her husband and their child."

"Yes, yes, naturally you are concerned," Dr. Brooks agreed, with evident relief. "And we shall talk about Tom presently, I promise you. But not just yet. Miss Winsham, please sit. I have something else to speak with you about first."

He sounded oddly nervous, and more confused than ever. Margaret allowed herself to be persuaded to sit in the chair Dr. Brooks had first indicated. Her gaze strayed back and forth between his face and the painting on the wall. And she waited for him to say whatever it was that was causing him so much trepidation.

Now it was Dr. Brooks who clasped his hands behind his back. He took a deep breath. He stared at her with the oddest of expressions upon his face. Finally he said, "Miss Winsham, I realize this may seem impertinent, but I wonder, that is, are you irrevocably opposed to the notion of marriage?"

"M-marriage?" Margaret echoed. He nodded. Now she took a deep breath of her own and tried to keep her voice from trembling. "N-no. Not irrevocably," she said.

"Would you be opposed to the notion of marriage with someone like me?" he persisted.

Dr. Brooks colored up as he spoke and sounded most unlike himself, Margaret thought. She had never heard him sound uncertain before.

But he mistook her hesitation and turned hastily away. "Forgive me," he said over his shoulder. "I have no right to put you in such an untenable position. It was a foolish notion anyway."

"Why foolish?" Margaret asked indignantly.

Brooks turned, a hint of hope in his eyes. He came toward her. "Because I am only a physician. To be sure, my breeding is perfectly good, but still, I know how most of society looks at physicians. What they think of us."

"I am not most of society," Margaret said gently.

He sat down beside her now and took her hands in his. His voice was eager as he said, "Yes, precisely! That is why I gave myself leave to hope that my suit might not be entirely unacceptable to you! Miss Winsham, do you think you could consider the possibility of marrying me?"

With creditable calm, she replied, "Yes, Dr. Brooks, I think that I could."

With what some would have considered a shocking

enthusiasm, he caught Miss Winsham up in an embrace and kissed her soundly. Margaret, despite knowing how improper this must be, did not object. Indeed, she responded just as enthusiastically as the doctor. Her arms wound around his neck and she threaded her fingers through his hair.

That was how the footman found them.

"Dr. Brooks?" the poor fellow said, his voice quavering. "The maid says the child is getting very restless and the tea is growing cold."

"To the devil with the tea!" Dr. Brooks growled in embarrassment.

"Yes, but not with Tom," Margaret reminded him.

She smoothed down her skirts as she rose to her feet, just as calmly as if they had not been found in such a compromising position.

"Thank you," she told the footman in a clear, cool voice. To Dr. Brooks, she said, "Are you coming, sir?"

"Yes, yes," he grumbled. "I suppose we had best send you back home with the boy, before his parents start to worry. I shall give you the mixture I've prepared, from which you can brew a tea for him. I shall bring you the tonic as well, as soon as it is ready. Mind, you are to let me know at once if he reacts badly to either. In fact, perhaps I had best come around tomorrow to see how he is doing for myself."

"Of course," Margaret said calmly, far too aware of the interested eyes and ears of the footman who still hovered in the hallway watching them.

The fellow got even more than he bargained for a moment later. "Of course," Dr. Brooks added with a frown, "you will need to show the child's parents how to give the tonic and how to take care of Tom, because once we are married, Miss Winsham, you will not be there to do so."

Was that a choking sound the poor footman made? He was almost certainly going to dash downstairs, as soon as he could, to inform the other servants of what he had overheard. And Dr. Brooks hadn't even noticed, Margaret guessed with an inward smile.

Just as he didn't notice the stir he caused, a short time later, when he informed his housekeeper that he was going to accompany Miss Winsham and the child home.

"Just to give the nursery maid my orders directly," he told her blithely.

From the knowing look on the woman's face, Margaret guessed that the footman had already spread the news. She supposed she had better start getting used to the twinkle in everyone's eyes and the sidelong looks. It was only going to get worse, she was certain.

The servants might not have been willing to wake Lisbeth and Thomas for Aunt Margaret, but they were not proof against Stamford and Rivendale and both of Lisbeth's sisters. Not when all four threatened to go above stairs and start opening doors until they found the one they wanted.

Lisbeth and Thomas dressed with some haste. They entered the drawing room to find the two men pacing and their wives watching the door with a grim look in their eyes. At the sight of Lisbeth and Thomas, both women flew to their feet and crossed the room to hug her.

"Are you truly all right, Lisbeth?" Alex demanded.

"They said you were kidnapped," Tessa added. "Did he hurt you in any way?"

Lisbeth shook her head. "No, I am fine." She paused and turned to her sisters' husbands. "I must thank you, Sir Robert and Lord Rivendale, for coming to my aid."

"Least we could do," Stamford said with a smile. "I am simply pleased to see you looking so much recovered."

"After all, Kepley once came to our assistance, you know," Rivendale added.

Thomas waved a hand, as though to signify it had been

no great matter. Stamford quirked an eyebrow upward and then said gravely, "Actually, that is another reason we are here. I spoke of it to you once before."

Now every eye in the room was on Sir Robert. "You did?" his wife, Alexandra, said with some surprise.

Stamford smiled at her and nodded. Then he turned back to Thomas. "Both last night and the time, two years ago, when Tessa and Miss Winsham were abducted, you showed great presence of mind. I spoke to you once before of certain possibilities, if you found yourself at loose ends. Have you given any further thought to the matter?"

"And I said then that my family would expect me to live the life of a gentleman," Thomas answered slowly. "After yesterday, I am more reluctant than ever to do anything that might put Elizabeth or anyone I care about in danger."

"Danger?" Lisbeth and Tessa echoed.

Stamford smiled. "I do not think there would be danger to you. Nor any real danger to Kepley or myself." Sir Robert paused and looked at Alexandra. "You know how important the work we do can be. You, yourself, encouraged me to stay on when I would have quit. Do you not think Kepley would be an excellent recruit for that work?"

Slowly Alex nodded. "You are quite right, of course." She turned and looked at both Lisbeth and Thomas. "Stamford has told me something of what you did while you were gone. And I do think he is right to suggest that you meet the man he works for. There are people who need help and matters just as important to be taken care of, here in England, as ever there were on the continent."

Thomas stared at her for a very long moment. "I see," he said at last.

He turned to look at Lisbeth, a question in his eyes. She nodded. "I think you ought to at least go talk to this man Sir Robert knows," she said.

"If you don't like what you hear," Rivendale added, "you can always refuse."

"Well, since you are all agreed," Thomas said with a feigned reluctance that fooled no one, "I suppose I ought to at least meet with the fellow."

They settled the matter between them as to when would be a good time. Then Stamford paused and said, with an apparent carelessness that was as transparent as Kepley's had been, "Is your father, the Marquess of Aylsham, at home?"

Thomas stared at him, but when Stamford added nothing more he merely shrugged and said, "Why don't we go find out?"

Five minutes later, Sir Robert found himself staring across the well-appointed study at the marquess and wondering if this was what he really wished to do.

Chapter 20

The Marquess of Aylsham rose to his feet at the sight of Stamford and his son walking into his private study together. Automatically his eyes went to a painting on the wall. When he looked back at them, he found the two younger men were staring at the painting as well.

"Who?" Stamford asked.

"One of my ancestors," Lord Aylsham replied.

"A remarkable resemblance," Thomas observed, staring from Stamford to the portrait and back again. "I cannot believe I never noticed it before."

"Leave us!" his father said sharply.

Thomas hesitated. Sir Robert nodded slightly and Lord Aylsham repeated his command. Kepley bowed and left the room. He was not even certain either of the other two men really saw him go. Behind him he heard only silence.

Sir Robert stared at the marquess, who stared back. Lord Aylsham seemed struck as dumb as Stamford. After a moment, the younger man cleared his throat.

"Thank you for agreeing to see me, sir," he said.

"Why are you here?" Lord Aylsham demanded, his coloring going both dark and ashen by turns.

Stamford hesitated, still stunned by the portrait that showed a face so similar to his own. But the marquess was waiting, and after a moment Sir Robert forced himself to speak. His voice, he noted, was oddly steady. "I came to see you, Lord Aylsham, because I thought I had reason to believe that you might be my father. It would seem I am correct."

He braced himself, waiting for the thundering voice that would declare him mad and demand that he leave at once! Stamford waited for the voice that would deny all kinship, despite any evidence to the contrary. But it didn't come. Instead, the marquess went more ashen than ever and grabbed for the edge of his desk.

When he spoke, Lord Aylsham's voice was scarcely louder than a whisper. "How did you find out?"

Stamford let out a breath. "I didn't believe it, not really, until this moment. Not until I saw the portrait—and your face. It was my wife—Lady Thomas's sister. She told me that you did not believe her sister's child was your grandson. She said it was because of a birthmark. A birthmark that all the male children in your family possess. And although I know very little about how I came to be placed in an orphanage, I do remember being told that when I was an infant, I had just such a birthmark at the base of my neck. So I came here today to ask you if it could possibly be true. I came to ask if I could possibly be your son or, if it was not you, if anyone else in your family might have been my father."

The marquess seemed to have been holding his breath, for now he let it out with an audible sound. His voice held more than a trace of pain as he said, "I could lie to you, but I shan't. I am your father."

Lord Aylsham paused and then added, "You had better sit down, Stamford. This might take a while to explain. I did not intend for you ever to know. I thought no one would ever need to know. I hadn't realized, you see, the remarkable resemblance to that particular ancestor of mine. Very few of us look like him, you know. But you are here, now, and there is no use in denying you the truth—whatever I may say outside this room to the rest of the world. I suppose I have no choice but to try to figure out how to make the best of all of this."

There could be no best of anything, Stamford thought. He wanted to scream the words aloud at his father. He wanted to curse him and tell Lord Aylsham the price his silence had cost him.

But he did not. Stamford had come for answers. Losing his temper would most likely deny him the possibility of being told what it was he most wanted to know. If he were thrown out now he might never find out anything at all about his mother. Odds were, the marquess was the only one who could tell him what he wished to know. So instead of shouting at or cursing his father, Sir Robert sat and waited.

Apparently the marquess understood because he took his own seat behind the desk again. Lord Aylsham clasped his hands together in front of him before he began. "Do you know anything about your mother?" he asked.

Stamford shook his head. "She was a dancer," the marquess said. "A very lovely creature, to be sure, but a dancer nonetheless. Scarcely someone to marry, even if I had not already been married to Lady Aylsham."

"Scarcely," Stamford echoed.

But the marquess did not seem to hear the sarcasm in his son's voice because he nodded and went on. "I am glad you understand. That makes matters easier. I gave her money, arranged the best of care, but she still died giving birth to you. One of the other dancers your mother knew took you to an orphanage. They thought it best because they knew, you see, that I could not have taken you in."

Again Lord Aylsham paused. "Of course not," Stamford said, knowing that his father would miss the sarcasm this time as well.

Something must have penetrated the marquess's awareness, however, for he frowned, shook his head, then went on, "Yes, well, at any rate, I was away, in the country when you were born. When I came back, the doctor who attended your mother simply told me that she had died. It was some time before I learned that you had not

died with her. And even longer before I was able to find
out where you were. Once I did, it seemed best to leave
you there until you were old enough to be sent off to
school. I did send you off to school; you cannot say I did
not do my best for you!"

Stamford wanted to laugh, and he wanted to cry. He understood, only too well, in the world in which his father
lived, the constraints the marquess would have felt were
impossible to ignore. And yet, he could not forgive or forget the years of deprivation or the struggles he had endured,
both at the orphanage and later at the school where he had
never quite fit in with the respectable sons of gentlemen.

"I understand that you did the best for me that you
thought you could do," he said at last.

It was enough to satisfy the marquess. "And you have
done quite well for yourself with the advantages I arranged for you. I am quite pleased, actually."

"I am so gratified to hear you say so," Stamford murmured.

That time an even greater ray of understanding must
have penetrated, for Lord Aylsham regarded Stamford
with a sharp gaze. "Do not be impertinent!" he said. "You
are fortunate I have done anything for you at all."

"One might argue the point, but I shan't," Stamford
replied, rising to his feet.

"Where are you going?" Aylsham demanded.

Sir Robert looked at him. "I came to see what sort of
man my father was. Now that I know, my curiosity is satisfied and I shall no longer pine for what I did not have."

Then, before Lord Aylsham could say anything more,
Sir Robert turned on his heel and left the room. Behind
him, the Marquess of Aylsham slowly lowered his head
into his hands.

Miss Winsham had been quite right to anticipate a
fuss. From the moment they walked into the Aylsham

town house, she and Dr. Brooks were greeted with a barrage of questions.

"Where have you been, Aunt Margaret?" Lisbeth demanded. "And why did you take Tom?"

"She brought the child to see me, at my request," Dr. Brooks stepped forward to reply.

He placed an arm around Miss Winsham's waist and ignored the shocked stares and the audible intakes of breath from those in the room. "Quite right of her, too. I've given Miss Winsham some herbs to brew into a tea for the child, and the moment it is ready, I shall be bringing around a tonic that may help. I can give you no promises, but it may help. If not, perhaps Miss Winsham and I can concoct something else, between us. Once we are married we shall be working together a great deal, I should imagine."

"Once you are married?" Lisbeth echoed, gaping at the pair.

"When did this come about?" Thomas asked, his voice a trifle more calm than his wife's.

Lisbeth peered more closely at the older woman. "Oh, Aunt Margaret, are you sure this is what you wish?" she asked. When Miss Winsham nodded, Lisbeth hugged her and said, "Then I am very happy for you!"

Eventually the uproar died down, and Tom had been taken upstairs and safely put into the care of the nursery maid, along with the tonic and instructions for its use. Then Miss Winsham and the doctor and Lisbeth and Thomas were able to talk. They had, she found, just missed seeing her other nieces and their husbands. That was a blessing for which she was profoundly grateful. Alexandra and Theresa, she thought, would have their own questions to be answered, but to face all of them at once would have been more than a trifle overwhelming!

As it was, there was an inquisition of sorts. Miss Winsham found she didn't really mind. Not when she knew it came from true concern for her. Not when she knew that

Dr. Brooks was the man she was meant to marry and the locket had been right once again.

She did finally manage to turn the tables and contrive to get Thomas and Lisbeth to tell her about their adventures the night before. When she heard what had happened, her own news paled by comparison.

"Is this man securely in custody now?" Miss Winsham demanded.

"He is dead," Thomas said in a curt tone of voice. "It was not what we intended, but he gave us no choice."

"In a way, I feel sorry for him," Lisbeth said to Thomas with a sigh. "I can only imagine how I would feel if something happened to you. And I know how angry I would be if I felt someone was to blame for it."

"Yes, well, we are not going to think of that today," he told her sternly, taking her hand and lifting it to his lips. "Today we are going to celebrate the wonderful news that your aunt and Dr. Brooks are to be married. When is the wedding to be?"

Miss Winsham and Dr. Brooks looked at each other. "We have scarcely had time to sort out such details," he said gruffly. "But I see no need to wait. To my mind, we have waited too long already. Much too long."

Then, as though it just occurred to him, Dr. Brooks looked at Miss Winsham to see if she agreed. She could not help but smile at the somewhat anxious look upon his face. She took pity on him and said, "Yes, of course we may be married quickly. As soon as the banns have been read. There is no one whose permission we need to ask, and no reason that I can see, to delay."

He squeezed her hand in delight. Thomas grinned. "Excellent. And do you mean to live in London or at your country residence, Dr. Brooks?"

This time the man looked to Miss Winsham first, quirking up an eyebrow in silent inquiry. She smiled. "I suppose," she said, "that we will divide our time between London and Dr. Brooks's country home—as he has been doing. Perhaps more time in the country, for I do not think the London air is good for his health."

"You do not mind?" the physician asked anxiously.

She shook her head. "Wherever you are, that is where I wish to be."

And if Lisbeth and Thomas had not been convinced before that the pair was well matched, that display would most certainly have persuaded them!

Thomas yawned and Lisbeth did so as well. Instantly Margaret scolded them. "You had no sleep last night—you ought to be in bed!"

Lisbeth blushed, recollecting that they had been in bed but not getting much sleep. But now she merely nodded and said, with a carelessness that deceived no one, "I suppose you are right. Now that we know you and Tom are safe, we ought to go back to bed."

"I agree!" Thomas said, with unbecoming fervor that put his wife to the blush again.

Even Miss Winsham and the physician blushed.

"Yes, well, er, I had better be going," Dr. Brooks said. "I do have patients coming around within the hour. I shall return tomorrow to check on my young patient again."

"I shall walk you to the door," Miss Winsham said, promptly rising to her feet.

Kepley and Lisbeth watched them go.

Chapter 21

Lisbeth would have followed Aunt Margaret and Dr. Brooks, but Thomas stopped her.

"I'm glad your son will have the best of care," he told her quietly.

Perhaps it was what they had been through, perhaps it was because she was so tired, but whatever the reason, Lisbeth lost her composure entirely.

"You keep calling him my son!" she said to Thomas, her voice shaking with anger. "But, whether you believe it or not, he is your son, too!"

"I have seen the birthmark on my nephews," Thomas said quietly. "I have seen it on every male child born to this family. Except on Tom. He cannot be my son."

He paused and looked at her, his eyes an icy blue as he went on, his voice bitter, "You said that there would be no more secrets or lies between us. You said no more hiding of what we fear most. But you will not trust me enough to believe that I would understand and forgive you, no matter who the father might be."

"Oh, I believe you," Lisbeth countered softly. "I believe you mean every word you say. But it does not change the truth that Tom is your son as much as he is mine."

They glared at each other, neither able to budge from what they believed to be the truth. That was how Lady Aylsham found them. She had opened the door without knocking. Now she came into the room and closed the door behind her, without asking if it was all right.

Thomas looked at her. "This is a private conversation, Mother," he said, holding on to his temper with obvious effort.

"On the contrary, it is a conversation that concerns me and always has. And I find that I can no longer be silent," the Marchioness of Aylsham answered as she came toward both of them.

She turned first to Lisbeth and said, "Forgive me, my dear. I should have spoken sooner but I was afraid. I thought this was a marriage of convenience, one in which it would not matter what my son believed."

"And now?" Thomas asked.

Lady Aylsham turned to her son. "And now I see that the truth does matter. I see how much damage my silence has done."

"What silence?" Thomas demanded. "Are you saying that you know something about this?"

The marchioness nodded, reluctantly it seemed. She was very pale and Lisbeth moved to stand a step closer so that she could put a reassuring hand on Lady Aylsham's arm.

"What is it you know?" Lisbeth asked softly, not wishing to startle the other woman.

But the marchioness looked at Thomas. There was a hint of defiance as well as apology in her eyes as she said, "I do not know for certain whether the child is your son. But I do know that he could be."

Thomas looked at her, wariness in his eyes. "But he lacks the Kepley birthmark," he said carefully.

Lady Aylsham seemed to gather up her courage. "So did you," she said.

For a moment, there was stunned silence in the room. Then Thomas made a gesture with his hand. "Impossible!" he said. "Someone would have noticed if I did."

The marchioness shook her head. She took a deep

breath and there was more than a hint of sadness in her
voice as she said, "It is not all that difficult to counterfeit
the mark—if one knows that one needs to do so and has
the help of a nursery maid who has taken care of other
children in the family and so knows how it should appear."

Lady Aylsham started shaking. Both Lisbeth and
Thomas urged the marchioness to sit in the nearest chair.
When she had done so, they sat on chairs facing hers.
That Kepley was stunned was evident from his face, but
he still reached out to take his mother's hand.

"Tell me."

It was an order more than a request, but Lady Aylsham
did not object. Perhaps she felt she had no right to do so.
Again she met her son's gaze with her own.

"I was unhappy. I was foolish enough to let myself be
seduced by a man who would have hurt your father if he
could. And he hoped to do so through me. But I didn't understand that until later."

She paused and for a moment there was a far-off look
in her eyes. Then the marchioness took another deep
breath and went on. "When you were born, Thomas, you
did not bear the birthmark. Your nursery maid and I
hastily made a counterfeit one. We were careful not to let
anyone else inspect it too closely. Our caution was well
merited. Not one week after you were born Lord Aylsham
asked to see the birthmark. He told me this enemy of
his—the man who had been my lover—had told him you
would not have it."

Lady Aylsham paused again. "Perhaps it was wrong to
deceive everyone this way. But I had discovered that I really did love your father and I did not think he would forgive me if he knew what I had done. And his enemy
would have enjoyed his revenge far too much. Besides, I
already loved you—too much to let you be disowned, as
I feared you might have been if anyone found out. So I
hid the truth. The mark fades, in any event, by the time a

child is two. We let yours fade a trifle sooner, but no one questioned that because it happens from time to time."

"Why are you telling me now?"

Kepley's voice was harsh and Lady Aylsham flinched at the sound of it. Still, she answered him. "I am telling you because you need to know, Thomas, that none of your sons will bear the mark. You need to know that the lack of a birthmark does not prove that Elizabeth has played you false. I believe, you see, that little Tom is your son. He has the look of you at that age and he has the same breathing troubles that my own younger brother had when I was little."

Thomas stared at her. He did not, could not answer, and Lady Aylsham turned to Lisbeth. "I am sorry, my dear. I should have had the courage to speak the truth before now. But I was afraid, so very afraid. I hoped that you might have a daughter and then no one need ever know."

"But why didn't you tell me to counterfeit a mark when my son was born?" Lisbeth asked.

Now Thomas found his voice. "She couldn't tell you," he said harshly, "because to do so would have meant admitting the truth, even if it was only to you. And my mother did not have the courage to do that. Instead, she turned our lives upside down. I am surprised she has the courage to tell us now."

Lisbeth fought to control her own emotions. There would be time enough for anger later. Now there seemed a more urgent matter to resolve.

"These breathing problems," she said. "They are common in your family? How are they treated?"

The marchioness shook her head. "A great many babies in my family are born with the same sort of illness as your son. Few of them live very long. No one knows how to make them feel better. You are fortunate that your aunt, Miss Winsham, has some skill in these matters."

Lisbeth could scarcely hide her disappointment. Lady

Aylsham seemed to mistake the reason for her dismay. "I know I should have spoken up," she said. "But you and Thomas had so little time together, after all. I thought it quite possible that you had indeed played my son false. Then, when he so unexpectedly returned, I hoped that my son would be as generous as he has been, and forgive you. I did not realize how much it would matter to the both of you."

Thomas stared at his mother as if she were a complete stranger. She stared back at him sadly.

"I deserve your anger," she said, "and I do not expect you to believe me. But I am telling you the truth today because I love you, Thomas. I have finally come to understand the damage my silence has done to you and to your wife and I wish to make amends. Whether you believe me or not, your happiness matters more to me than my own."

He could not answer her. The bitterness in his eyes was so strong that both Lisbeth and Lady Aylsham flinched. Thomas rose and turned his back to his mother. He began to pace the room.

"Is this supposed to make me happy?" he flung over his shoulder at the marchioness. "Am I supposed to be delighted to discover I am not my father's son?"

"You are his son in his eyes. He will never know otherwise unless you tell him, and that will be your choice," Lady Aylsham answered evenly.

Now Thomas stopped and looked at his mother. "He knows," he said flatly. "Looking back, I think he must have known right from the start. It explains why he was always impatient with me, why he was always so certain that I would never make him proud. It explains why he did not object when I purchased colors, nor tried to stop me from going off to war. Not the first time and not after I was injured."

Lady Aylsham gave a tiny cry of protest. "He could not have known! He would have told me if he did."

"Are you so certain, Mother?" Thomas demanded.

"Perhaps he loved you enough that he did not wish to cause you distress or risk an open breach either."

She was very pale, shaking her head in denial. Thomas was shaking his as well, but in disgust. Lisbeth sat watching both of them, filled with dismay and thinking matters could not get any worse. She was wrong.

The door opened again and this time it was Lord Aylsham who stood on the threshold. He seemed somehow to have aged greatly since that morning. All three of them stared at the marquess, unable to speak. He advanced into the room and eyed them shrewdly.

"A family conference?" he asked. "And no one included me? Let me guess as to what it might be about. Perhaps the question of the child's paternity?"

"Have you been listening at the door?" Lady Aylsham asked, resignation in her voice.

He nodded and looked even older. "But I heard nothing I did not already know. You were quite right about that, Thomas," the marquess told his son.

"Why did you never say anything?" Lady Aylsham asked.

Lord Aylsham came over and took her hand. He held it for a moment before he answered, his voice low and filled with pain. "Thomas had the right of it. I said nothing because I loved you and feared that an open breach between us might drive you back into your lover's arms. Because I wanted you at any price, including pretending that I believed Thomas to be my son. Because I knew, you see, that I had given you cause to be unhappy, though that was never my intent."

The older man paused and looked at Thomas, who had not moved from the moment his father walked into the room. "I am sorry. I ought not to have taken my anger out on you. It is just that I always found myself looking for signs of your real father in you. I kept expecting to find proof of the same weakness of character, the same streak of irresponsibility, and the same immorality that was so much a part of him. It wasn't there, but I kept looking all the same."

Thomas could not answer and the marquess clearly did not expect him to try, for he turned to Lisbeth. His face was lined and drawn, and his voice was weary as he said, "I owe you an even greater apology, my dear. I, too, knew that the child—if it were a boy—would be born without the mark. But I could not say so. For if I admitted that to you, then it would have been as good as admitting I had been cuckolded and that Thomas was not my son."

Lord Aylsham paused and rubbed a hand over his eyes. He looked tired, so very tired. He forced himself to go on. "It was not right, but I dared not wait until the child was born. I spoke first and accused you of being unfaithful to my son. I was angry anyway that he had defied my wishes and refused to marry the bride we had chosen for him."

"I am told you even tried to have the marriage undone!" Thomas said sharply.

"Yes, I did," the marquess said. "I meant to bring you back to England and make you marry Anna Dalwood. But then you were reported lost at sea and it was too late to tell the *ton* that I had changed my mind and decided your marriage was a valid one after all, even if I had not been worried the child might be born without the birthmark."

Lord Aylsham turned back to Lisbeth. "I am sorry, my dear. Like my wife, I wish to make amends. And we will do so. We will make it unmistakable to the *ton* that your marriage to Thomas has our blessing and that we believe your child is his son."

It was Lady Aylsham who then asked, "Can you forgive us? Either of you, or both?"

"No!" Her son's voice was harsh and laced with anger.

Lisbeth rose to her feet and walked over to Thomas. She placed a hand on his arm, but turned to face Lord and Lady Aylsham.

"I do not know if we can forgive you," she said honestly. "Your malicious tongues have cost us a great deal. And your attempts to have me cut off from the funds Thomas left for my care, hurt my son as well as me. I might have forgiven you for myself, but it is much harder for me to forgive what you did to my child."

With each word, the older couple seemed to shrink in upon themselves. Lisbeth felt sorry for them, but the pain of what they had done to her and to Tom was still too strong for her to be able to forgive. She looked up at Thomas.

"We are both tired," she said softly. "There will be time to talk about this more at a later time. For now we ought to get some rest."

He nodded, and together they left the room. In the hallway, they noticed a number of servants hanging about; all of them no doubt hoping to discover what had gone on. Neither Thomas nor Lisbeth were about to tell them. Behind them, Lord and Lady Aylsham closed the door and Lisbeth could hear the murmur of voices as the marquess began to tell his wife what he ought to have told her years before.

Upstairs, Lisbeth was grateful that they had the privacy of their room. No one would intrude here this time, not once they locked the bedroom door at any rate.

"What shall we do about your parents and what they have done?" Lisbeth asked.

Thomas looked at her. "Precisely what we have been doing," he said. "Letting the *ton* see that we are devoted to each other, that I am devoted to Tom. We will reconcile with my parents because an open breach would only cause the gossip to continue. But it will not be easy for either of us, I think. Or for them."

Lisbeth nodded. Thomas drew in a deep breath. He pulled her into his arms and kissed the top of her head.

"I, too, must apologize," he said. "As much as my heart told me that you were telling the truth, as much as I saw of myself when I looked at Tom, I could not let myself believe he was my son. Can you, will you, forgive me?"

Lisbeth hesitated. She wanted to refuse. The hurt of his distrust still ran very, very deep. But then she thought of the marquess and his wife. How they had acted out of pain instead of being honest with each other and in doing so wasted so many years when they might have comforted each other instead. She knew she could not bear it if her marriage ever took such a turn. So now she took a deep breath of her own and looked up at Thomas.

"I am hurt that you did not believe in me—or your son," she said. "But I understand. And because I do, I can and will forgive you. It seems to me that we have lost far too much time already to anger. I am not willing to lose any more. Nor to risk that we should ever end up like your mother and father. I meant what I said, earlier, when I said that I wanted us to be a shelter for each other. That means even when it is difficult for us, not just when it is easy."

She kissed him then and that kiss was plea and promise and passion all combined. She felt his arms tighten around her and she smiled.

Thomas broke the kiss, then, and his voice was husky as he said, "Neither am I willing to repeat the mistakes my father and mother have made. And I swear to you that we shall make up for all that time lost to anger. Tom will be a much-loved child, Elizabeth. And together, with Dr. Brooks and your Aunt Margaret's help, I promise you that we shall find a way to help our son."

She touched the side of his cheek. This was where she belonged, she thought. To kiss Thomas again came as naturally to Lisbeth as did the loving him that followed.

Afterward, when they were lying together, she said softly, "Tell me about France."

And he did.

Chapter 22

"Is she ready yet?" Alex asked Lisbeth.

"Aunt Margaret is still packing up her herbs," Tessa replied.

"Well, the carriages are waiting," Thomas said impatiently, "and it is time for us to leave for the wedding. Dr. Brooks will be wondering what on earth happened."

Lisbeth shook her head. "No, I think he will understand, for I suspect he would be just the same. That is one reason they will be such a good match for each other."

"I hope you may be right," Tessa said doubtfully. "But it is just so hard to imagine Aunt Margaret married. She has always told us that she never wished to marry. Indeed, she always told me that she could not abide the though of having to live with any man."

"Well, I think it is wonderful that after all these years, she has found someone to love," Alex told her sisters. "And that it was his face she saw in the locket, so many years ago."

"I wonder what would have happened," Tessa said, "if Aunt Margaret had not been away when Dr. Brooks came with Dr. Parr to treat Mama, all those years ago. Do you think they might have liked each other then? What would her life, what would our lives, have been like if she had been married to him all these years?"

Lisbeth shook her head. "Things happen as they are supposed to happen," she said firmly. "I am sure there was a reason Aunt Margaret and Dr. Brooks had to wait to find each other all these years."

"Do you think so indeed?" a tart voice interrupted their discussion. "You may well be right, but I do not intend to stand about here all day! No, nor keep Dr. Brooks waiting at the church for me a moment longer than necessary. Come along and stop dawdling, girls!"

"Of course, Aunt Margaret."

"Right this way, Aunt Margaret."

"The carriages are waiting. I promise you we shan't be above half an hour late, Aunt Margaret."

"Nonsense! We shan't be late at all if no one delays us needlessly," Miss Winsham retorted. "I know precisely how long it takes to drive there."

She fixed a minatory glare upon each of her nieces in turn. But a smile trembled at the corners of her mouth and she could not keep up the pretense for more than a moment.

"Oh, how I shall miss all of you!" Miss Winsham said. "Are you certain I am doing the right thing?"

"Yes!" three voices said as one.

"Of course you are doing the right thing," Thomas said soothingly.

"You and Dr. Brooks will be very happy together," Rivendale chimed in.

"But we really ought to be going," Stamford added. "The poor fellow must be nervous as it is, waiting for you. You don't wish him to think you have changed your mind, do you, Miss Winsham?"

Still she hesitated and Thomas held out his hand to her. "You are a beautiful bride," he said. "And Dr. Brooks is very fortunate to have you. I have no doubt you will keep a lively household and argue over a great many things. But I also have no doubt you will make each other very, very happy."

Miss Winsham stared at him, then slowly reached out and placed her hand in his. "Then let us be going," she said, a softness to her voice that none of them had ever heard before. "I don't want to keep him waiting any longer."

Despite the teasing words of her nieces, Miss Winsham was not, after all, late for her wedding. Everyone was just on time. And it seemed to Lisbeth and her sisters, as they watched the couple take their vows, that they had never, excepting themselves, of course, seen a better-matched bride and groom than Aunt Margaret and the doctor.

The locket at Lisbeth's throat grew warm and she touched it lightly. She found herself wondering what her daughter—if she had a daughter—or her sisters' daughters would make of it. Would it help to lead them to their true love as it had done for Lisbeth and Tessa and Alex and Aunt Margaret? She hoped so.

Wish Always With Love. It was something to live by, she thought. And that lesson alone was something she would be grateful for, all the days of her life.

Author's Note

This is the end of my "magic" locket series. I hope you enjoyed the adventures of the Barlow sisters. Next, look for another Miss Tibbles story. Colonel Merriweather is asked to help catalog items from the war for the British Museum. Naturally, since Miss Tibbles is involved, nothing goes as expected!

Look for news of upcoming books at my Web site:

www.sff.net/people/april.kihlstrom

I love to hear from readers. I can be reached by e-mail at:

april.kihlstrom@sff.net